Georgina Scott was born in the county of Norfolk, England, to Thomas and Sylvia who relocated from London in the early 1970s. She grew up surrounded by the beauties of East Anglia.

Joining the Royal Air Force in her late twenties, where she met her husband Charlie, also a serving member of the Royal Air Force. Both now settled in rural Lincolnshire with their beloved pets, Rose and Muggs.

After leaving the Royal Air Force and continuing to work within the aviation industry, her old passion for writing was reignited.

Charlie, with love.

Georgina Scott

ECHOES IN THE WOODS

Mue,

Hope you enjoy

with love

Georgina Scott.
x

AUSTIN MACAULEY PUBLISHERS™

LONDON · CAMBRIDGE · NEW YORK · SHARJAH

A CIP catalogue record for this title is available from the British Library.

ISBN 9781788480109 (Paperback)
ISBN 9781398433960 (ePub e-book)

www.austinmacauley.com

First Published (2021)
Austin Macauley Publishers Ltd
25 Canada Square
Canary Wharf
London
E14 5LQ

First and foremost, I would like to say thank you to my darling husband, Charlie, for believing and encouraging me to fulfil my dreams in becoming an author. My dear friend Nick Lund, thank you also for giving me the encouragement to persevere. To Greg Browne, you know what you did. I would also like to thank Austin Macauley for taking a chance on me. Thank you all.

Chapter 1

"One of these days, I am going to kill you, kill you slowly and before I bury you, I am going to watch you burn!"

Jake thought to himself, as he sat strapped, sore and naked, to a crate in his own mess and blood, in a dark, foul, stinking room, just off the basement: his punishment for the night along with ten lashings of his father's belt.

This morning, he was caught killing a lamb. He was curious and wanted to know what it felt like, compared to insects and amphibians. The slippery warmth of flesh against his skin felt extraordinary, exhilarating. Hearing the lamb choke and gurgle, gasping for air as he slit its throat, then cut all the way down to its stomach, it took about thirty seconds for the lamb to die. Pulling the skin apart, the first thing he noticed, was how warm the inside of the body felt, pressing deeper inside, feeling his way around the rib cage, organs and muscles. He was in total ecstasy. Heart pumping out of his chest as the adrenalin rushed around the body. It was the first time he felt a sensation within his groin. He felt excited!

The moment wasn't long lived as he felt a hand grab the back of his neck, shaking him back to reality. "You bloody fucking little bastard!" he said, dragging Jake back to the house, in his deep, gravelled voice and cursing the boy as they crossed the field.

His mother, Faith, was a good-looking woman, with an hourglass figure and naturally curly dark shoulder length hair; she was exceptionally kind, friendly and very funny. People were naturally drawn to her. She knew what to say, and how to say it. Men drooled over her and women were envious and jealous, but they all loved being around her. She didn't have a nasty bone in her body. In her boys' eyes, she was exceptional.

She was hanging out the washing when she saw Jake being dragged and punched by his father and came rushing to his aide, only to be pushed and thrown to the ground. You could hear her cries and screams as she begged him to let the boy go. He grabbed her by the throat whilst covering her face with spittle and said, "Stay out of this and shut your mouth woman, or else so help me."

"Please John, he's just a boy, you are hurting him, let me see to him," she said in a trembling shaky voice.

"I don't think so," he said, again pushing her to the floor.

He throws Jake, front forward, over some hay bales, removes his belt and starts lashing. On the third strike, Faith drags herself up from the ground and throws herself on top of the boy, with the belt striking her face, she screams in pain in floods of tears. "For god's sake woman!" he shrieks, getting angrier by the minute. He grabs her arms and pulls her off of him. "I won't let you hurt him, I won't John I won't," she says, inconsolable. Fighting him with her fists and kicking with her feet. He grabs her by her hair and punches her, knocking her unconscious.

His eyes changed to cold daggers as he looked upon the boy, who can feel the anger, the hatred, the rage, and should be scared, but he is not. The disdain he has for his father cannot be explained. It took eight lashings before he whimpered and that seemed to appease his father as he looked down on the boy with a grin. Jake never showed really how much he hurt. His father grabbed his skinny, tiny arm and dragged him down to the basement, told him to take his clothes off and then strapped the boy to the crate with rope and here he sat strapped, waiting for the door to open, waiting for his mum, but she didn't come. He didn't even look at Jake or say anything to him, just turned and walked away closing the door behind him. Jake didn't give his father the satisfaction of pleading and begging like he had done in the past; there was no point, as it always fell on deaf ears.

The room was big enough to accommodate four people comfortably; it was cold, dark, dirty and dank. The mould odour was enough to make you sick; there was no light, natural or otherwise. It was a place where wooden crates and other materials were stored. The only person that would come down to the basement was his father; his mum always said the basement gave her the creeps and went down there as little as possible, and even then, would take one of the boys with her.

The basement scared Jake to death; he swore blind there was something else in that room with him. He would have nightmares and bed-wetting for weeks afterwards, waking up in the middle of the night in sheer terror after feeling a coldness of breath against his neck, unable to move, paralyzed to the bed.

John walked up the stairs and closed the basement door mumbling and cursing the boy under his breath. He walked to the kitchen and took two swigs of Jack Daniels. He looked out of the window and saw Faith still lying unconscious on the ground. He exhaled a deep breath and walked out of the house over to Faith and carried her back into the house and up to the bedroom.

After tending to her face, he sat on the edge of the bed bent over, with his head in his hands. Faith started to stir; she placed her hand onto his back and started to cry, "Where is he, where is Jake?"

"In the basement," said John, in a slumbering voice.

"You can't keep doing this John. You're hurting him, this is getting out of control, and you're not like this with the other boys."

"I'm sorry, I can't help myself. I have tried to love, accept him, but I can't. I just can't. Every time I see or look at him, all I see is Robin. He has to go; I want him out of the house. I have said it before and now I am saying it for the last time."

"Let me speak to my parents first."

"You do that; either they take him or he goes into a care home. Either way, he has to go."

"Please, let me bring him up from the basement? I can't bear him being down there all on his own, in that horrible place," said Faith in a quiet, whispering voice.

He nodded and looked into her eyes, "I'm sorry." Tears ran down his face; she pulled him to her and they kissed. Their tongues entwined. She pulled him on top of her, running her fingers through his hair. He kissed her sore face. "You are so beautiful; I am so sorry, I love you so much!"

He spread her legs, running his fingers up her inner thigh, her knicker gusset was moist. He applied pressure to her clitoris whilst entering her with his fingers. Her soft groans stiffened his cock. He removed his white t-shirt and dark blue jeans. He cupped the back of her legs and pulled her to him. Ripping her cotton knickers off, exposing her soft flesh, moist with anticipation, he separated her outer lips with his fingers; he kissed and licked her vulva, drinking in her scent. She tasted of peaches, nibbling and sucking her clitoris, her groaning deepened, asking for more as her fingers ran through his dark blonde hair. "Come up to me, baby!" said Faith.

Removing her clothing, he made his way up her body, kissing and touching as he went, exposing her hard erect nipples. Seeing them made him smile as he said to himself, "Nipples like scammell wheel nuts," massaging her pert breasts with his hands whilst licking, flicking and sucking her nipples. His cock was so hard now, it throbbed and ached for her juicy wet pussy.

Their mouths touched hungrily as he slipped his hard throbbing cock into her very wet tight pussy. They groaned in unison as he pumped. Her hands slid down his back and cupped his buttocks, squeezing and smacking his butt cheeks, her finger reached and inserted into his anus. He became even more excited and pumped harder, deeper and faster into her delicious pussy.

With her body shaking and grinding against his, "More, John, more," was what Faith said. Together they rolled and he was on his back with her straddling him. Riding his shaft, his hands squeezing her breasts, her hand cupping his balls, gently squeezing and massaging, he brought himself up to her and placed one of his arms around her, with his hand on her butt cheek caressing her anus and the other holding her face with his fingers, holding her hair back. She came down to him and their mouths entwined. Both their bodies climaxed and orgasmed together, John spilling his seed inside of her and Faith gushing, soaking him and the sheets.

Faith lay there in his arms, listening to him fall asleep, as his breath slowed and deepened. She carefully got off the bed, so she didn't disturb him, and then placed the duvet over him to keep him warm from the cool breeze entering the bedroom from the slightly ajar window. She got dressed as quickly as possible and made her way down the stairs to the basement.

Before she opened the door, she got a fleece blanket from the closet. She opened the door and saw Jake, tied to a crate, naked, with tears flowing down his face. Her heart saddened and broke. She rushed to him and wrapped him in the fleece. "I'm sorry, Mummy," said Jake as she untied the ropes on his legs. She pulled him to her and hugged him and they both cried together as she wrapped him in her arms.

"It's me that should be sorry; I should have taken you away from this place a long time ago. O, my baby boy, I am so, so sorry! I love you so much," she said, as she kissed, cradled and rocked him in her arms.

Faith carried him upstairs to the bathroom, where she ran him a warm bath. She tended to the wounds on his ankles, where the ropes had been tied too tight, leaving sore broken skin. She tenderly applied a wet cloth to his bruised and battered body. He whimpered and flinched at every touch she made, which brought tears to her eyes.

She passed him his toy boat, hopefully to try and take his mind elsewhere, away from the pain. "I am going to take you away from here," she said wiping his face with a flannel. "I am going to call Nana and Gramps to come and get you. Jake, would you like to live with Nana and Gramps?"

"Will you come too, Mummy?"

"No baby, I have to stay here and look after your dad and brothers, but I will visit you often," with tears in her eyes knowing she was lying to him. John would never allow a visit.

She dried him off and put some fresh pyjamas on him and put him to bed; he was asleep in moments.

Faith called her father. After an hour of an argumentative conversation, he agreed to come and get Jake, and said he will be with them by tomorrow morning.

It was 3 o'clock in the afternoon and Faith was late in leaving to go and collect the boys from school. She phoned the school and apologised to Mrs Rose who agreed to stay behind with them until she got there. It took forty-five minutes before she pulled up at St Benedict's Catholic School. Faith got out of the car and thanked Mrs Rose, a tall thin woman, always dressed in bright florals, colourful from top to toe; she was pleasant, amiable enough, but always looked at you like she had shit under her nose. Faith hugged and kissed all three boys, apologised again, then returned to the truck.

Matthew, the eldest of the four boys, would be fourteen this year; he had his fathers' ocean blue eyes and dark blonde hair with an adventurous nature and loved the farm, always helping out, wanting to know the ins and outs of everything. He noticed straight away her marked face, but didn't say anything; he just gave her a big hug and helped his mum put Henry and Mark into the truck and then they set off back to the farm. "Jake is going to live with Nana and Gramps," said Faith, holding back the tears.

"O," said Matthew, then paused and continued to say, "maybe it's for the best mum, the house has been in a turmoil since he was born." He said staring out of the window.

"That is not fair Matthew. What happened was not his fault!"

"Maybe not, but Mum, he's not right!" said Matthew looking at her.

She pulled the truck over to the side of the road, "You explain that, Matthew!"

"All I am saying is, he isn't like us, or like any of our friends."

"He is only eleven years old. How can you say that about him!" said Faith, trembling, knowing it is true but not wanting to come to terms with the idea that Jake is different.

"He hurts things, mum," said Mark and Henry looking at each other.

"What things? What are you saying? Oh my god, he is only eleven years old!" Faith said in disbelief.

Finding it very hard to accept what her boys were telling her, she learned of the killing of insects, frogs and birds. Mark and Henry told her that he hurt them by pinching, biting and kicking them when no one else was around and that they are afraid of him. "You're both lying and making all this up. What you are telling me is that Jake, my son, your brother, is some kind of monster," said Faith placing her head in her hands, shaking her head in disbelief, unable to digest what was being said to her.

"Mum, what we are saying is that he needs help, not Nana and Gramps, that won't help him," said Matthew, but all three boys together said, "He needs the people in the white coats." Then, in unison, significantly, waved their fingers in a circular motion at the side of their head.

She restarted the ignition and they made their journey back to the farm; the truck was quiet all the way with no one saying a peep until they got home. She told the boys to sit at the kitchen table and do their homework. She made her way upstairs to the bedrooms, firstly, to check in on Jake who was still fast asleep. She stroked his hair and kissed him on the forehead then told him she loved him. Then she checked in on John who wasn't in bed. Making her way back to the kitchen, she heard the tractor in the distance and asked Matthew to go and tell his father that dinner will be ready in one hour.

Matthew ran from the house towards his dad and caught his attention; he saw him ploughing the top field. His father waved out of his window and told Matthew to stay put in hand signalling. He turned the tractor off and got out and made his way over to Matthew. When he was close enough, Matthew ran to him and wrapped his arms around him, hugging him tight. "I love you, Dad," said Matthew.

"I love you too, Son," he said, squeezing him tight.

"So, what has happened, Dad? Mum is upset and she says Jake is going to live with Nana and Gramps," said Matthew, looking up to his dad.

"It's not been a good day, Son."

As he sat on the ground next to Matthew, both stared at the half-ploughed field, talking about the day's events, with his arm around one shoulder. "I'm glad he is leaving. I do love him; after all, he is my brother, but I just don't like him. I've tried to like him, get on with him in fact, include him when we play. It's hard, it's just so bloody hard," said Matthew.

His dad looked down at him and it dawned on him that his fourteen year old was growing up and way too quickly for his liking.

They picked themselves up, dusted off and headed back to the house. Teasing and wrestling with each other as they went and not realising that in the distance looking through a window was an eleven-year-old boy watching them. Emotions ran full throttle through Jake's body, envious, jealousy, hatred, longing and wishing for that same contact, but he knew deep down it will never be; it will never happen.

Chapter 2

It was 10:30 am by the time Mac and Mary arrived at the house. Jake was sitting on the porch steps, looking sullen. Henry and Mark ran out of the house and hugged their grandparents and started to tell them bad jokes. Matthew stepped out of the front door and sat next to Jake. "You okay, creep?" said Matthew, giving him a slight elbow. Jake just nodded and shrugged his shoulders. "Just think of all the places you're going to see. Wish I was going with you," said Matthew. Mary approached and kissed both boys, then headed into the house with Mark and Henry.

Mac sat next to Jake and winked at Matthew. Jake got all sullen and became very tearful. "What are my ears hearing? Crying? Is that tears I am seeing!" said Mac as he picked Jake up and placed him on his lap. Jake started to giggle as Gramp's beard started to tickle him; with one hand, Gramps tickled him then lifted him and blew raspberries on his tummy. Matthew was startled as he heard his little brother's laugh, as it was not something he had heard often, and then they all laughed together.

They heard raised voices from the house. "Go and play with all your brothers. I will send out the other two," said Mac to Matthew, then got to his feet and went into the house, rubbing his hands on top of Jake's head as he went.

Henry and Mark came running out with their wooded swords, shouting, "I'm gonna be Skywalker."

"No, I am," and so on, until Matthew interrupted, "I will be Solo and Jake will be R2D2. Henry, you're Wookie and Mark, you are C3PO." For the first time in a long time, all four boys played as they should.

John and Faith sat at the kitchen table with her parents, drinking coffee with a mid-morning snack. "So, you think Jake will be better off with us, do you? Let me finish, Faith," said Mac raising his hand in mid-sentence. "Yes, you're right. Yes, he will be better with us, because let's face it, you both have done a bad job in raising, caring and loving him. This has not been a stable home for him and I still haven't finished Faith," said Mac thumping his fist on the table.

With a raised voice, "Now we love you daughter, but the treatment of Jake is abominable. You have allowed your husband to abuse a child in ways I dare not think about," said Mary.

"But Mum, Dad," said Faith looking bewildered at her parents, only to be shaken to the core by their coldness towards her. "Don't you Mum, Dad us! I have never, in all my days, wanted to raise a hand to you or any child no matter how angry or frustrated I was. So, you tell me how this has happened? You both agreed to raise Jake, to love, protect, so what the hell has happened?" said Mac waiting for an answer.

Both Faith and John exchanged looks, "It's me. I can't accept him Mac. Every time I look, hear or see him, all I see is Steve's face. I want him gone, one way or the other; if you don't take him, he will be put into the care system," said John adamantly.

"And this is what you want, Faith?" said Mary

"No. I want him here with us, with his family," said Faith, with John glaring at her.

"Faith, this is not what we agreed," said John.

"I know, but I can't let him go. He is my baby boy," breaking down in tears.

"Faith, this needs to happen, he needs to go," said John glaring at her with looks that could kill.

"John, please don't do this," said Faith, pleading.

"What the bloody hell is going on here?" said Mac, with a raised voice.

"Faith, Faith," said John sternly.

Faith tried to compose herself. "I'm okay, it's just a bit too much," wiping tears from her cheeks.

"So John, to appease your damaged ego, you want to get rid of Jake. Do you really think removing him will solve your problems?" said Mac.

"No, but something has to give Mac, and I hate the little bastard. I can't stand the sight of him."

"Jesus Christ. So you decide to take your anger and revenge out on an innocent eleven-year-old boy, who was the product of what happened, but not the cause! Damn it, John! You brought that man into this house! You, you instigated all this!" said Mac pointing a finger and then thumping his fist on the table. Then he continued to say, "Well, boo-fucking-ho," getting up from the table, then walked outside and played with the boys for a while to calm down.

"I have never seen your father like this before, Faith," said Mary then reached out her hand and placed Faith's hand in hers. "Are you sure you want to do this because you have to be sure," Faith looked at John, then hesitantly nodded.

After a breather and a stretch of the old legs, and some more tea, the four of them carried on talking. Faith and John tried the best way to explain to her parents that Jake was mentally unstable and that she didn't want to admit it until she picked up the boys from school. Then went on to say what they had told her, "Dad, you are the best person to help Jake. You are a professor of Psychiatry, this is your field; if anyone can help him you can. Dad, the boys are scared of him!"

"He is eleven years old Faith, boys will always fight and scrap," said Mac.

"We know this Mac, but he has started to kill animals now. He slit a lamb's throat and to its stomach, he made a right mess. I know I have done wrong but the boy can't stay here, Mac!" said John.

"Very well, he will come home with us. Make sure all his things are packed because he will not be coming back, ever," said Mac, with a bad taste in his mouth, again walking out of the kitchen into the front yard, and called Matthew.

"Gramps, I'm coming," said Matthew, running out from behind the shrubbery towards his grandfather, giving him a big hug and cheesy grin.

"Let's go for a stroll and a chat shall we, and you can fill me in on everything that has happened, okay?" said Mac.

"Yes, Gramps."

It was forty minutes until Mac and Matthew returned back to the house. "Mary, I think it's time we got back on the road. It will be late by the time we get home," said Mac.

Mary got Jake's belongings into the truck then went up to her daughter and hugged her, "Are you sure you want to do this?" said Mary again.

"Oh Mum, no, but what can I do. I fear for him if he stays here."

"I love you. Take care of yourself, my darling girl, we will see you soon and don't worry he will be fine with us," said Mary, giving Faith another big hug and kiss. Then went and hugged and kissed Matthew, Henry and Mark.

"Jake, be good now for Nana and Gramps, I love you my darling baby boy," kissing, hugging and touching him, with tears in her eyes, as though it would be the last time she would lay her eyes on him.

Calling the other boys over to say goodbye, they all had a group hug, "See you later creep," said all three boys. Jake looked over to see where his father was, and saw him standing on the porch steps with his arms crossed. His father just stared at him, then turned around and walked back into the house.

Mac saw the exchange between the two of them; this sent a chill down his spine. "Right, okay. Let's go, Jake," said Mac. Jake ran towards his nana and they both got into the truck.

Mac approached Faith, wrapped his arms around her, "We will take good care of him, baby girl."

"Oh, Daddy!" she said crying. "I will phone him every night, I promise."

"Make sure you do. I love you," said Mac, walking towards the truck. Waving goodbye, Mac, Mary and Jake headed for home. Faith watched them drive away cradling her stomach. In floods of tears she fell to her knees, inconsolable, distraught. Matthew, Henry and Mark hugged and squeezed her tight.

John approached the huddled group. "Go, play now, boys. I'll see to your mum, she will be alright," bending down wrapping his arms around her. Faith tried to push him away but couldn't, and instead, sobbed into his chest and squeezed him tight. "I'm sorry, I'm sorry, baby," said John, kissing the top of her head, holding her tight in his arms.

It was another hour before John and Faith headed into the house. John put Faith to bed then came down stairs and made a late lunch, putting Faith's lunch in the fridge for later. John and the boys sat down for lunch in silence. After lunch, Henry and Mark played outside for a couple of hours then watched television before heading to their bedroom; Matthew helped his dad tidy up the kitchen then decided he would go and read his comic in his bedroom.

Fatigue hit John like a bolt; he secured the house and headed upstairs to check on Faith. She was fast asleep; her face was puffy from all the crying. John wrapped himself around her and entered into a deep sleep.

Chapter 3

Ella McPherson lived two doors down; she was also eleven years old with brown, long curly hair. She and Jake hit it off straight away and very soon became inseparable, best friends even. She would read stories to him and then help him to read also. They would play hide and go seek and in and out of each other's houses. Climbing trees, they also made a den out of wood and fallen branches in the back yard of Ella's house, a sacred place, and all adults are barred from going into the den.

Ella and her mum made wind chimes and placed them all over and around the den. Whilst Jake got an old sleeping bag he found in the loft, he asked Mary to help him clean and wash it, and then placed it into the den. Mac found a plastic tarpaulin about twelve feet square in his garage and wrapped it around the den to protect it from the elements. It was a good solid den.

At first, Jake was intimidated by Ella's dad, Graham; he was tall, very broad. His muscles looked like they had exploded from his body, but he was a fair, kind man, always had a smile, a very funny man. Over the coming months Jake started to feel at ease with him. Graham and Mac collectively built a barbeque and seating area next to the den, where both families came and spent time together. They got on well.

As they got closer, over the coming months, Jake opened up to Ella on how he was subjected to physical and mental abuse from his bullying father and how he was treated very differently compared to his brothers. He showed her his healed scars on his back, wrists, ankles, thighs and abdomen. It seemed that there wasn't a day that passed without him getting into trouble and his father relished in his punishment, always berating him for the slightest mistakes calling him 'stupid', 'dumb' and 'bastard'.

He told her how his mum tried to protect him, but in doing so, she was also beaten to a pulp and he would still be punished but more harshly. They lived on a two hundred acre farm and kept dairy cows, chickens and goats. They also grew crops and strawberries, rows and rows of strawberries.

He told her of his nightmares which had now quietened down since living with his grandparents. He shared his feelings of self-doubt, hopelessness and helplessness. "I will never let anything hurt you again, you are safe here with us, we will look after you," said Ella, hugging him tightly.

He kept the bed-wetting and the voices he heard in his head to himself; it was just too embarrassing to admit. He also kept to himself about the vivid dreams of tying up Ella, her naked beautiful body against crisp white cotton sheets, biting her soft silky skin, drinking her blood from the fresh opened wound whilst he entered inside of her.

Chapter 4

Life had changed dramatically on the farm. Faith and John were getting on better, the tension and stresses in the atmosphere had almost cleared. Mark and Henry now had a room of their own. The past six months had gone so quickly since Jake left with her parents. Faith kept her word and she phoned Jake every night to ask how he was and what sort of day he had had. He also sounded for the better; he told her about Ella and the den they all made and the day trips, which he enjoyed.

Faith stayed upbeat in all her conversations with Jake, whilst at the same time overcome with sadness. She was especially sad on this one occasion as Jake had a birthday; he was now twelve years old.

John and Matthew were cleaning up for dinner, "Dad?"

"Yes, Son."

"Can we go and see Jake, Nana and Gramps; I kind of miss them?"

John sort of stared out of the window. "Dinner is ready; let's eat," whilst thinking that he would never set eyes on that boy again as long as he lived. They walked into the kitchen where their dinner was already on the table.

John was about to sit down when he looked at Faith standing at the sink. He noticed she had changed into her summer dress. As the sun shone through the window, the light lit her up; her dress became see-through, the silhouette of her pink fleshy bottom sent his heart racing and his groin hard and throbbing.

The boys sat and ate their food while John went up to Faith and wrapped his arms around her and gave her a big squeeze whilst rubbing his groin against her bottom. He moved her shoulder length soft dark naturally curly hair and kissed her neck and drank her in, he loved the smell and taste of her.

His hand lifted up the front of her skirt and rubbed her clitoris, whilst his other hand was squeezing her breast. "You're so sexy, so beautiful," whispering in her ear, then kissed her neck.

"John, please baby, not in front of the boys."

"You're soaking, you're so fucking wet. I want you, baby I want you." He swung her around, taking her into the utility room, shutting the door behind them, then quickly undoing his trousers, pulled out his hard cock and started to fuck her up against the butler sink.

Faith could never resist him, nor tried to stop him or wanted to. She grabbed his hair pulling his head back, hearing his deep groan as she kissed him on the neck working her way up to his lips, exploring every inch of his mouth.

His hands still cupping her bum cheeks, ramming his cock up deep inside of her until they both climaxed together; Mark and Henry started to giggle, snigger as they could hear their parents having sex, but Matthew couldn't listen and put his finger to his left ear to block out some of the noise. He told the other two boys to quickly finish their dinner, as he knew what the consequences would be if they didn't. Once done, all three boys quietly, quickly disappeared up to their rooms, until they were called back down.

Chapter 5

Mac and Mary arranged a camping holiday, with the invitation extended to Ella. Her parents jumped at the chance for her to go, with a new baby about to come into the world, they desperately needed some alone time.

They packed up the caravan and headed off to the National Park, where two days of activities were on the agenda, walking mostly. "Nana, which part of the National Park are we visiting?"

"This year we are visiting and staying at Eckerts Creek. Listen, I shall read from the website," she said.

She was about to go on and read from the website when Ella interrupted, "Will we be seeing birds and fish?"

"Yes, Ella, we will first park up, and then we will go for a walk to see some of nature's beauty. Today will be a lazy day, and then tomorrow we shall be canoeing for part of the day," said Mary.

"Canoeing? Never been canoeing before," said Ella and Jake.

"First time for everything," said Mary, looking at Mac with a smile.

"When will we get there, Nana?"

"We will arrive around 10:30," said Mac.

They followed the signs to Berri, missed Sturt Highway for access, so they continued via Lower Winkie Road, which lead to Eckert's Creek. They kept driving around and from what could be seen, there was one toilet for campsites 1-17 and another toilet for campsites 18-40. The pit toilets were well kept but it all depended on the amount of visitors, as the busier the location, the smellier the pit toilets would be and then they rapidly kept deteriorating with cleanliness and smell over time. Luckily, Mary and Mac thought of everything and had a chemical toilet.

It was 10:45 am by the time they found a spot to make camp. They chose an area where it was easily accessible to the river, no steep banks. It had a little beach to access the water, which made it easy for the canoes and kids to enter and exit the water without any dramas. It also had privacy and shade, it was the perfect spot.

As Mary and Mac set up camp, Ella and Jake went to explore. They played and swam in the water, and when they weren't playing and swimming in the river, they had lots of fallen logs and bush land to play, making up imaginary games and friends.

"Ella, Jake, come on, we are going for a walk," Mac called out. Both of them came running towards him, laughing. "Get your hats, and put on your ruck sacks. Make sure you fill your water bottles," said Mac. Mary put together some wildlife spotting sheets. They split into pairs, boys against girls. The boys went ahead but not too far, just so they couldn't hear each other's answers.

The girls decided that they weren't very good at spotting and naming birds and insects, but were okay on fish and mammals. The boys, however, were a lot better at spotting and named everything on the sheets. Once they had finished and the kids started to lose interest, Mary took the sheets and placed them in her rucksack so she could tally up later on who are the winners and who are the losers, which come with a forfeit and the winners get a prize.

Meeting back up, they continued for another hour before deciding to turn back. Ella and Jake held each other's hands on the way back, laughing and joking. Mary and Mac hooked each other's arms and walked behind, "What do you think Mac, are those two made for life?"

"Who knows, they have a lot of growing to do yet."

"Well, I think they make a cute match."

"They are only twelve and eleven, behave woman! Anyhow, he has a long way to go; he still hasn't opened up about what happened on the farm."

"It's only been six months Mac; he is still bottling his feelings up. He is still bedwetting, three days out of seven now, I am not going to make a fuss of it. He knows we are here for him and he will open up but in his own time. We have to give him that."

"I'm still very angry with Faith; how could she allow this to happen. It's been six months and no visit. Yes, she phones him every day. At least she kept her word on that!"

"Yes, I agree with you there. Do you think there is something in it with what they said about Jake not being right?" said Mary.

"Not sure, but I do believe Matthew. That boy is too old for his own good."

"Well! I have been watching Jake, checking his room and stuff and I see no signs of anything for us to be alarmed about. Maybe he was killing things to release the tensions and frustrations. I mean let's face it; he was being beaten, violently badly beaten. He had no one to turn to and we don't know how long it has been going on and to what extent. Give him time Mac!"

"I'm afraid, now that Jake has been removed from the farm; I have dread in the pit of my stomach. I fear for Faith and the boys!"

"Are you saying that Jake was a barrier?"

"Yes, and now that obstacle has been taken away, I am worried."

"Oh Mac, John loves Faith and the boys, I really don't think he will hurt them."

"I do hope you are right babe, but I can't help the way I feel. There is something very wrong. You didn't see the exchanged look between Jake and John; it sent chills down my spine."

It took an hour and a half for them to get back to their campsite. Ella and Jake changed back into their swimwear and played in the river. Mac sat reading his book whilst Mary prepared the meat for the barbeque; the bread rolls and salad had already been prepared.

They all sat down for dinner around the barbeque, talked and sang songs. Watching the sun go down then the stars started to appear in the sky one by one; Ella and Jake changed into their pyjamas whilst Mary made hot chocolate. They stayed up one more hour before sending them to bed.

"I see no signs that Jake is unhinged babe," said Mac.

"Like I said, you have to give him time; he will open up and then, when he does, we will face it head on," said Mary.

"Let's go to bed babe, I'm tired," with that Mac put out the campfire and they both headed into the caravan and went to bed.

Chapter 6

Mark and Henry were in their beds fast asleep and Matthew was in his bed reading Marvels, the war of the realms, where all ten realms have fallen to Malekith and his army. He was distracted by a sound of a vehicle approaching the house really fast. He turned off his side light and peeked through the curtains. He knew his dad had gone out for the evening to a local farmers meeting. He realised it was his dad in his truck, driving erratically before the accident, where he hit a tree. Running out of his room, down the stairs and out the front door, towards the car, he saw that his mum was already at the scene, pulling his dad out of the truck. She turned, "Matthew, help me grab his legs."

He was a dead weight. They managed, between them, to get him in the house and onto the couch. "Mum, is he going to be okay?" with tears bursting from his eyes.

"Yes, darling, he will be fine, it looks far worse than it is. I will call Dr Moody and see if he will make a house call, just to check your dad out. Now go back to bed," hugging and kissing him on the forehead. "I swear baby he will be okay, now go to bed." With that, Matthew turned and headed back upstairs but didn't go into his room. Instead he sat on the top stair with his knees into his chest.

It was nearly an hour before Dr Mitch Moody arrived. "Hello Faith," longing for her touch.

"Hello, Mitch," running her fingers through her hair and as her breathing became heavier, she looked him in the eye.

"Drunk again, is he? I see the truck is well parked? Well, let's give him the once over," placing his bag next to the couch, he examined John. "Would you like a cappuccino, Mitch?"

"Yes, please," watching her as she walked into the kitchen, putting the kettle on the stove.

Twenty minutes passed and Mitch walked into the kitchen. "Well, he will live. A mild concussion, just keep an eye on him. He will wake up with a saw head, I dare say!" taking a gulp of his cappuccino.

"How have you been Faith; how are things?" putting down his cup looking at her with those big brown eyes. "Things have been better. John has been better, but he has started drinking again," looking at the floor.

"I heard about Jake. Have you seen him?"

"No, not for six months, but I phone him every night. He had a birthday, you know," holding back tears.

"You haven't seen him for six months, bloody hell, Faith."

"It's been difficult."

"For whom Faith, certainly not John."

"It's difficult, Mitch. Tensions eased when Jake left with Mum and Dad, the house seemed almost back to normal you know, how it used to be before the rape."

"I thought you guys moved on from that?"

"I thought so too. I have, John hasn't. I think with Jake being here it was a constant reminder."

"Now you're making excuses for him. He was the one who brought that fucker into your home and never listened to you, just bloody oblivious to it all, until it was too late," taking a deep breath. "So what's his excuse now?"

"What do you mean?"

"Well, Jake has gone, so that obstacle has been removed and yet, he hasn't changed, back on the booze and still beating you. Is he beating the boys as well?"

"No, no he isn't. Mitch, you don't know what you're talking about, he doesn't hurt me and he wouldn't touch the boys."

"Bullshit Faith, who the fuck are you kidding. I can see the faded bruises on your neck; they are probably about four weeks old," said Mitch, running his fingers down her neck.

"Mitch, I love him. He is the father of my kids, please don't do this."

"You don't love him, you're scared of him!" said Mitch taking a breath. "You said those words to me once. Damn it, Faith! I have never stopped loving you; you are the first thing I think about in the morning and the last thing I think about at night. We haven't seen each other in months, I miss you!" brushing his thumb over her lips whilst holding her head in his hands.

"Please Mitch, don't! I can't do this with you. I really need you to leave, please!" she said in a whispering like voice.

"Okay, I'll go. You know where I am and how to get hold of me," pulling her closer and kissing her passionately on the lips, wrapping their arms around each other.

She walked him to the front door and said goodbye. They both kissed again, and then he left. She shut the door, turned and headed into the living room to check on John. She looked over him and breathed a heavy, deep sigh. She sat in her chair and carried on reading her book.

Matthew sat at the top of the stairs trying to process what he saw and heard. He felt confused and not sure what to do… He quietly got up and headed back to his room, shut his door and got into bed; he tried to hold back the tears, wiping them away with the back of his hand. Within minutes, he fell asleep.

Chapter 7

"Wakey-wakey, rise and shine," Mary said, pulling the covers off the kids. Mac was already up and about, preparing breakfast whilst singing. "Come on you two, we are canoeing today," said Mac. Prising themselves from their beds, rubbing eyes and yawning, making their way out of the caravan. "What time is it?" said Ella.

"It is almost 9:30 am, so sit down and eat up, bon appetite," said Mac, walking off, chuckling to himself.

Ella and Jake just looked at each other, then both looked at Mac walking with a skip in his step, singing and whistling; they both burst into laughter. Mary looked on at all three of them as she was pottering around the campsite and smiled to herself.

"Right, you two, once you are done, go wash your faces and brush your teeth then get dressed, shorts and t-shirts, I think," said Mary, as she prepared the rucksacks.

As she was tidying away the breakfast cups and plates, Mac was getting the canoes ready. Both kids were dressed and put on their buoyancy aids and headed towards Mac, with Mary shortly behind them. Before setting off in the canoes, Mac ran through some health and safety features with the kids as it was their first time in a canoe and on the water.

"Now, we are not going very far, but you will see plenty of wildlife. Ella, you're with Mary, which leaves you with me Jakie boy. Okay, let's get going."

The river was about thirty metres wide. They took an upstream route which was winding with low flows; the steep grey banks had redgum trees along the top which provided the banks with magnificent shade. It was a pleasant winding route. The further upstream they went, the scenery changed in areas from grey to sandy banks; there were also patches of young redgum woods.

"Look, Mary what's that bird? Jake, do you know what it is?" said Ella.

"Well, if you listen you can hear it whistle," said Mary.

"I know, I know, it's a Whistling Kite, and also known as a Whistling Eagle," said Jake.

"Oh, well done, Jake, that's my boy!" said Mac, chuffed as punch.

With Jake, smiling from ear to ear, after hearing praise from his granddad; for the first time in his life, he felt like he belonged and was happy. They saw many species of wildlife, from Kangaroos to water birds, Parrots and reptiles. They were out on the river for almost four hours, only stopping for lunch which they had in their canoes, Ella and Jake took many photographs. It took another two hours to get back to the camp at slow pace. Once there, Jake helped Mac with strapping the canoes to the sides of the caravan, whilst Ella helped Mary with prepping dinner.

Jake and Ella ran around playing chase, and hide and go seek, and then they both sat on a fallen tree branch and Ella began reading 'The Adventures of Huckleberry Finn'. Jake put his arm around her and gave her a big squeeze; she turned her head and looked at him. Once dinner was served, they all played Pictionary and then they all took turns to read aloud a chapter from 'Huckleberry Finn'. Mary made hot chocolate and then they all settled in for the evening.

The morning was bright, the sky blue and not a cloud to be seen, the sun was already high in the sky. The usual breakfast routine got underway. "As this is our last night here, would you both like to sleep outside in a tent tonight?" said Mary.

Both Ella and Jake looked at each other, then both said in unison, "Yes, please."

"Good," Mary said.

"Will you and Gramps be with us Nana?"

"No darling, we will be in the caravan, those days are long gone, for me and your gramps!" Both kids just smiled at each other.

Once breakfast was over and done with, giving an hour for the tummies to settle, all four went swimming and snorkelling, and then played Dolphin Relay Race. As Ella was a really strong swimmer, she was really excited with this game and her competitive nature came out in leaps and bounds. Jake was a little apprehensive as he had not played this game before.

Mac explained the rules: "You see that point," pointing his finger, "well, that's the turning point, there and back in the fastest time. Each person pushes the ball to that turning point and back again, however, you are only to use your forehead or nose. You are not allowed to touch the ball with any other part of your bodies or you will have to return to the start and start all over again. You, then, pass the ball to the second person waiting at this end, then continuing until all have completed three turns each. How does that sound?"

"What teams are we on?" Ella said.

"Well, as I see it, you and I are the strongest swimmers Ella, so we will compete with each other and Mary and Jake will compete."

"Sounds good to me, boys against girls," the rest of them said, with Ella and Mary giving each other the high five.

"Jakie boy, when me and Ella are in position, you do the ready steady go, now are we all ready, say YEAH!" said Mac, thrusting his fists in the air.

"YEAH," they all repeated and did the same.

Both Ella and Mac positioned themselves in the water with the balls just in front of them. Jake then shouts out, "Are we ready?" both Ella and Mac shouted back, "YES!"

"GO!" Both Jake and Mary shouted out encouragements for their teammate. Both swimmers chose the breaststroke, both neck and neck, and then Ella headed out in front by an arm's length and was the first at the turning point. Mary and Jake positioned themselves, still shouting for their other teammate. With Ella in the lead, passing the ball to Mary, she head-butted the ball and off she went.

Jake was a little slower, starting off once Mac passed him the ball. Now getting in the swing of things, Jake was catching Mary. He caught her at the turning point, with Mac shouting, "Good lad, Jake, keep going!" Jake was in the lead now by a leg length, tapping the ball with his nose. Mary managed to lose track of her ball as she head butted it out of range and had to go after it, which put her and Ella way behind. Ella put her hands on her head with disappointment and frustration, "Mary, we are gonna lose, quicker!"

With Mac looking at Ella, shaking his head with a chuckle, Jake came into reach, then passed the ball and off Mac went. Mary managed to get the ball back on track, with Ella itching to go at it. Mary passed the ball. There was no way Ella could catch Mac but she did manage to close the gap between them.

Jake felt his right leg twinge, but thought nothing of it. As Mac passed him the ball, Jake set off again. He got to the turning point and was half way back to Mac when his right leg cramped. Jake went into a fit of hysterics, splashing and crying out. Mac immediately went to Jake's aid and so did Mary, both reaching him. Mac turned him over onto his back and swam him back to the bank. With Jake crying in pain, Mac laid Jake down with his leg out straight; he then pulled the top of his foot towards Jake's head and held it there, until the cramp subsided.

Ella swam out to get both balls, and brought them back to the bank. "Is he going to be okay?" said Ella

"Yes, he will be fine. It's a cramp, he's got," said Mary. After the cramp subsided, Jake felt a little pain and tenderness in his right leg.

"Okay, Jakie lad, keep your foot like that whilst I massage your calf muscle. You let me know if you feel your muscle pull again," said Mac, with Jake nodding with his head. "How's that?" said Mac, with Jake giving him the thumbs up. "Okay, let's get you on your feet!" and with that Mac pulled Jake to his feet, "there you go, it will be tender for a while so nothing too strenuous, slowly walk around and you will be fine in no time," said Mac.

They all got dried and dressed. Ella and Jake walked around hand in hand laughing and joking just being stupid. Whilst Mac and Mary put up the tent, then got the kids to get and put their duvets and pillows inside the tent with a battery-operated lamp. As night fell with the same routine as before, pyjamas and hot chocolate before bed; Ella and Jake were excited about sleeping in the tent.

Mac and Mary said goodnight to the kids and watched them go into the tent. "Now, no messing about you two, off to sleep," said Mary.

Both Mary and Mac broke open the beers, "I've seen a change in Jake this weekend," said Mary.

"Yes, I have seen it, too."

"Do you fancy drinking up and then get an early night, babe?"

"Yes," Mary said. They sat in silence and drank the rest of their beers. Mac took her hand and led her to the caravan where they made love and fell asleep in each other's arms.

Ella, putting on the lamp giving off just enough light gave Jake a shove, "Jake, Jake!"

"What?"

"It's my birthday next month; will you come to my party?"

"You woke me for that? Of course, I will."

"Jake, Jake!" giving him another shove.

"What now?"

"You are my best friend and I love you."

"I love you, too," and pecks her on the cheek; they fell asleep holding each other's hand.

It was still dark when Jake woke suddenly from a nightmare. He dreamt he was back at the farm in the basement in that dark dank stinking room. He wasn't alone, the voices were with him, talking to him, echoing each other. Telling him to kill them, kill them all.

Jake held his head and shouted out, "No, no I won't."

Stirring Ella in the process, "Jake, you okay." She sat up and put her arm on his. He was shaking, cold but sweating. She put the lamp on and held him tightly, "It's gonna be ok," she said to him.

It was early and the sun already had heat in it. Mac and Mary left the kids to sleep as they got themselves ready and packed up the camp in readiness to start their journey home. It was cereal for breakfast all round and a cup of Yorkshire Tea. Mac had the tea sent over from his cousin who lived in Sheffield, England.

Mary woke the kids and gave them breakfast whilst Mac put away the tent. She told them to brush their teeth, wash their faces, and they didn't have to change out of their pyjamas as they will be staying in the truck with no diversions planned.

She noticed they were a little subdued and out of sorts. "You guys ok?" she said.

They both nodded, "We didn't sleep very well last night," said Ella looking at Jake. "Well, then you can sleep on the way home." Once they were all packed up and a quick tidy up of the camp, both kids slept in the back seat of the truck for most of the journey home.

Chapter 8

After dropping the boys off at school, she noticed Matthew was not his self, "You okay, darling?"

"Yes," replied Matthew before getting out of the truck and just walked off in the direction of his school friends. He didn't acknowledge her or say goodbye like he usually does. She frowned and thought to herself that she would speak to him after school.

Saying goodbye to Henry and Mark, kissing them both on the cheeks, "Ooh, Mum do you have to? My friends are watching." They both said, then walked through the gates towards their friends who were blowing kisses at them jokingly.

Faith thought, *Kids,* then got back into her car and headed into town towards the doctors surgery where she knew Mitch would be at the surgery. She had to see him, and doing so, made a double appointment with him so no one would get suspicious. She sat there, reading a magazine, but not taking in any of the celebrity gossip. She heard her name being called. She knocked on the door and heard Mitch say, "Come in." She walked in and shut the door behind her.

"Hello," they both said in unison. She pulled the chair around so she was close to him and directly looked at him, her heart skipped a beat as they both stared at one another. "I never got to say the other night, that I missed you too and I am sorry for shutting you out but I feel I owe you an explanation as to why I stopped being with you," reaching out, her hand entwining their fingers together.

Mitch started to talk, "No don't, Mitch, you need to listen. I didn't stop seeing you because I didn't care or stopped loving you. It was because John needed me, my boys need me. John was hurting Jake more frequently whilst being a doting Dad to the other boys. I had to make a choice and I chose them. I was being selfish with you, putting my own needs before theirs; hopefully, time will make him change and he can find resolution."

"He doesn't want to change Faith. I still stand by what I said, leave him, you and the boys can come and stay with me. We will get Jake back from your parents and be a family. Leave him, Faith, for your own sake as well as the boys'."

"I can't, I wish I could be with you but I can't, you don't know him, he scares me! I have made my bed; he would never let me take the boys away from him. For the sake of my boys, I have to stay. I'm sorry."

Both Mitch and Faith put their foreheads together and cried. Mitch pulled Faith onto him and they both held each other close and tight. "I love you," Faith told him. She could feel his hardness swelling within his trousers as she straddled him. Kissing his cheek, making her way towards his lips, they embraced. She undid his trousers, feeling his hard penis in the palm of her hand, applying pressure she slid her hand up and down his shaft before slipping him inside of her.

He carried her to the examination table, still inside of her; he lay back on the table with her on top of him. She undid the buttons of her dress revealing her perfectly formed pert breasts. Both hands covered her tits and he squeezed them, her nipples stiffened and he brought himself up to her, suckling and nibbling then, whilst she pumped his cock inside of her.

His girth filled her; the more excited she became, deeper inside of her, he went filling her up. His hands were caressing her buttocks, rubbing her perineum with the tips of his fingers, feeling her inner lips move up and down his shaft. His balls were soaked with her juices. He lifted her and carefully placed her underneath him. She brought her legs up and onto his hips as he slid deeper inside of her, pumping harder and faster. Groaning with every thrust, her hands in his hair, their lips met and melted together, tongues entangled. The harder he pumped, the wetter she gets. Bodies in ecstasy, heavy panting, her body shook beneath him, feeling her cum squirting all over his penis, sending him over the edge, spilling his seed deep inside of her.

He was still lying on top of her, touching her face, telling her how much he loved her. Tears started to run from her eyes. Concern came over his face when he saw her; he scooped her up and held her tight. They stayed holding each other.

Their intimate moment was interrupted by a tap at the door. "Dr Moody," then there's another tap at the door, "Dr Moody," the person said.

"Shit, shit! Get dressed babe," said Mitch quickly pulling up his trousers and tidying himself, he pulled the screen around the examining table and then went and sat down at his computer, "Yes, Kate, come in."

The door opened and walks in Kate, the practice secretary. An ageing woman of about sixty-three but she still had her looks. She had been with the practice for over thirty years; there wasn't anything Kate didn't know about, but she was extremely discreet and never gossiped, and she knew Mitch as a boy when he came into the practice with his father, then taking over the practice, when his father retired. She knew about the affair between Mitch and Faith. He confided in her. "Sorry for interrupting Doctor, but I really need your signature for these letters, before the morning post leaves," said Kate.

"Very well," holding out his hand for the letters, he signed them, then handed them back to her, "and there you go, Kate."

As Kate shut the door, Faith pulled back the curtain. "Well, that was close," she said, not knowing that Kate was aware of their situation.

Mitch wrapped his arms around Faith again, squeezing her tightly, "Faith, before you go baby, I have something for you," with that he handed her a mobile phone, an old black Nokia. "It only has my number on it, just in case you might need it."

"Mitch, I can't accept that. If John ever found it, there is no way I can explain it."

41

"I will sleep better at night knowing you have it. Hide it in a place somewhere safe and don't tell anyone. Please."

"Okay, thank you," with that they both kissed and she left the room.

Chapter 9

The camping holiday seemed so long ago. On one of the rare occasions, Ella walked home from school alone; Jake had to leave early and as it was only a mile from home to school, Ella said to her mum that she would walk home. After some considerable persuasion, her mum finally gave in and said it was okay for her to walk home alone.

She crossed the road and passed a group of boys and girls who were a year ahead of her and joined the path. As she walked down Steep Hill, she heard a rumbling behind her. She turned her head to see what sounded like rolling thunder and before she could react, she was thrown off her feet. She held her arms out straight and braced for the impact.

She felt her left wrist crack, the pain shot up her arm, then she let out an almighty scream. It took a few moments to register that she was screaming. Her rucksack hit the back of her head then slumped off to one side. As she tried to get up from the floor, someone grabbed her hair and swung her around. She fell to the floor but was still being dragged by her hair. She felt her tights rip and her knees welled up in pain. Then she felt a kick in her legs, then more kicks.

When they let go of her hair, she put her head in her hands and curled up into a ball. She was continuously kicked and punched throughout her body. Somebody grabbed her head and banged it on the concrete path. All she could hear was laughing and being called foul horrible names.

The attack lasted for what seemed forever. She heard a car stop. "OI!" someone shouted, then her attackers fled, running away laughing and saying, "We gonna get you!" In floods of tears, her saviour helped her to her feet, not realising that it was Mac that was helping her to her feet, until she lifted her head and wrapped her arms around him, clinging to him and wouldn't let go. She was shaken to her core and looked white as a ghost. She had a grazed and bloody face. "Ella, let's get you home," said Mac, holding her tight.

Jake was at the car watching the group run away, thinking to himself, "I know who you all are." Jake pulled her close to him, squeezed her so tight and kissed her forehead. They sat next to each other on the back seat. Jake could feel her trembling body, and his t-shirt was soaked in her tears. Mac pulled up in the drive, got out of the car and knocked on the door to Ella's home. "Hi Graham, sorry to be the bearer of bad news but Ella's been attacked by a gang of kids."

"What the fuck," Graham said rushing to the car. Ella's mum, Josie came waddling to the front door, now heavily pregnant. "Mac, what's happened," said Graham with concern. "Ella's been attacked by a group of kids," said Mac. "Oh my god," Josie said, waddling as fast as she could to the car.

Graham opened the car door. "Ella baby," he stopped in his tracks and was totally shocked at what he saw of the state of Ella. "D–d, Daddy, oh Daddy," Graham scooped her up in his arms and took her into the house. Everyone followed. Josie gasped as she saw her little girl. "Oh my god," she kept saying under her breath, as she followed her husband. Graham sat Ella on a chair, sobbing her little heart out; he examined her wounds from head to toe. "She needs an x-ray on her wrist and maybe her head. There is a nasty bump to the top of her forehead. She has broken skin on her knees and shins. So, baby girl, let's get you to the hospital and we will get a real doctor to give you the once over, okay," said Graham to Ella. She nodded but was still sobbing. "Mac will you give us a lift, mate?" said Graham.

"Yes, yes I will. Jake you head home and tell your nana where I am heading, okay Son?" said Mac.

"Okay, Gramps," turning and about to walk out the door when he turned and looked at Ella in distress, feeling helpless and overwhelmingly guilty because he wasn't there with her, blaming himself as he headed for home.

Mac, Graham, Josie and Ella waited at the hospital in Accident and Emergency for about twenty-five minutes before being seen by Doctor Ashram. "Hello, I am Dr Ashram," he said, shaking Graham's hand with an Irish accent. "Well, now, what happened to you?" said Dr Ashram.

"I was beaten up," said Ella tearfully.

"Well, then, let's give you the once over, and see if we can use some magic to get you better, ok?" he says.

"Ok," said Ella, with a nod, still holding onto her father.

Dr Ashram started with the bump on her forehead. "That's a nasty bump you have there."

"It hurts."

"I'm sure it does," as he checked her eyesight and then checked her painful wrist.

"I don't think it's broken but we will send you for an x-ray, just to make sure," he then checked out the condition of her knees and cleaned them up.

"Okay Ella, we will get you up to x-ray to check out that wrist."

Ella's wrist was fractured but not broken; the nurse applied the plaster to Ella's arm and asked her what colour she wanted. Ella had chosen pink; she was to wear the cast for up to six weeks. They also x-rayed her head and the doctors saw no problems or any underlying issues, other than that Ella was going to have a nasty bruise for a while and a headache. Doctor Ashram told her parents to keep her awake and if she became drowsy with sickness, to bring her straight back. They prescribed her with medication for pain relief, but other than that, just kept an eye on her.

Once she was allowed to go home, her dad scooped her up and they all left for home.

Chapter 10

Jake was beside himself with worry and rage, pacing the living room, and kept looking out of the window waiting for his grandfather's car to pitch up. All sorts of images and thoughts went through his head, from having a blood clot on the brain to an amputated arm.

"Right, that's it, Jake. Will you sit down and calm yourself? She will be alright."

"You don't know that Nana, anything could have happened!" again looking at the window.

"Jake, I insist you sit down and calm yourself. I won't say it again!"

Reluctantly Jake sat down, Nana noticed he was shaking and twitching. She put her hands in his and said again that she will be okay. Jake just nodded, holding back the tears.

"I'm gonna get them Nana, all of them, the ones who hurt her, you'll see!"

"Okay Jake, now calm yourself," with her arms outstretched inviting Jake into her arms.

"Oh, Nana, I feel so helpless," jumping into her arms.

She held him tight, consoling and comforting him. When they heard Mac's car pull up in the drive, Jake pulled out of Mary's arms and ran outside, with Mary not far behind.

"Is she going to be okay? How is she?" said Jake all flustered and stressed.

Graham got out of the car and said, "She will be fine Jake, she has a fractured wrist and a nasty bump on the head but in time she will be fine."

Jake helped Ella out of the car and saw the pink cast, "It's pink; I didn't know they do colours."

"I didn't, either," Ella said and gave him a smile with a hug, "I'm okay, Jake."

"I'm gonna get them, all of them, the ones who did this to you."

Ella pulled herself back and just looked at him.

"Come on baby girl, let's get you in the house. You can see Jake tomorrow. Thanks Mac, for everything," Graham said and led Ella and Josie into the house.

"No worries, Graham. Goodnight all," then took Jake by the shoulder and went indoors.

Jake was a lot calmer now that he knew that Ella was going to be okay. They sat down for dinner and once finished, Jake excused himself and went to his room. He took out his textbook and wrote in the back the names of the six kids that hurt Ella.

Justin McClure
George Bradshaw
Heather Cilliërs
Kevin Stones
Wilf Macintosh
Natasha Cley

Chapter 11

Three weeks had passed since the beating. Jake walked Ella home from school without fail. They never saw the group of kids, so came to the conclusion that they were keeping a low profile or were off beating someone else up, but that didn't stop both of them from being on edge.

Jake enrolled in kick boxing classes which took up an hour of his time, three days a week, but he didn't care. He felt more confident and stronger walking down the street protecting Ella. He knew that even at this stage in his training, he could hold his own against those kids. Once he walked her, he would give her a hug and a kiss on the cheek, then off he went to gather intelligence on the six. He would make sure he was back in time for training and dinner; his timings were spot on, making no one suspicious.

Jake looked at his list and decided to start from the top, gather as much information about Justin McClure and the others as he possibly could. However, his thoughts couldn't help but take a side step onto what is or what was he going to do to them once he set his plan in to action. He knew he was going to scare them. Maybe that was going to be enough, but then he thought, no, they hurt Ella, for no reason whatsoever and they are going to pay for what they had done. He wanted them to feel pain, be scared and know what it is like to be terrorised.

Determined now more than ever, he swiped a writing pad from school. He made sure he would keep up with his studies so as not to attract any suspicion, though some days that was really difficult. He found an old gym bag and green balaclava in the loft; he placed his black trackies, trainers and balaclava in the gym bag and hid the bag in the den for now, knowing that it would have to be moved at a later date.

On his way back from training, looking at his side window, he noticed an abandoned warehouse. It was less than two miles from school but then he thought how he would get them there without anyone spotting them, so he dismissed that location. He then thought of the woods at the back of the school. Perfect!

Once he finished his dinner, he asked if he could go out for an hour. Mac and Mary agreed and told him to take his mobile phone. Jake ran all the way up the steep hill, past the school and into the woods. He could hear the voices, telling him to kill them all. He steered off the path placing markers. He marked out six trees by carving the initials into the trunk. At the last tree, he carved JM into the bark then stood back, he figured the first victim should be the farthest away.

Later that night, before he went to sleep, he grabbed his writing pad and wrote down nine items that he was going to need to put his plan into action:

Location
Bungee, Rope, knife
Torch, Gloves,
Large Handkerchiefs,
Blindfolds and Tape.

Jake went back to the woods over a period of days to get to know the route, terrain and layout, until it became second nature; he placed the rope, handkerchiefs, blindfolds, the bungee cord with plastic coated metal hooks on both ends, and tape, in a plastic bag at the base of every tree and covered it with leaves. He took out his writing pad and ticked off the items on his list as he said them over in his head. He managed to get some of the items on his list from school with the exception of the bungee cords, which he took from the garage at home.

He stood back taking in the moment feeling proud with what he had achieved so far. Fully satisfied Jake made his way home.

Chapter 12

Justin McClure is a fat ugly boy with bulbous eyes. He never stopped eating and he was unfit, flabby and farted a lot. He lived on St Giles Road, Number 14 with his father who looked like a dead head, fat and unshaven, very scruffy looking. He wore trackie bottoms that were hanging down from his arse and a t-shirt that was torn with a can of beer in one hand. Jake also noticed there was lots of shouting in the house; as soon as Justin walked in, he was shouted at. With his younger siblings screaming, there was no peace, no quiet. The house was untidy and so was the garden.

Jake kind of felt sorry for him because he was easily led and manipulated and took the blame for the group. He didn't have any choice; it was take the blame or get beaten up every day, just like what they do to others and he would rather be part of the group than not. At least no one would mess with him or cause him any trouble. In his mind, it was a case of survival and he felt the group made him look cool and he felt accepted and part of something.

Jake didn't notice any kind of violence, just really loud noise coming from the house on most days. Volume on both the television and stereo system were turned up full blast. There was conflict between neighbours on both sides; the neighbour on the right, banged on the McClure house screaming to turn the noise down, then there was a confrontation between both men, both exchanging un-pleasantries towards one another.

When it got really heated, the police turned up, dissolved the conflict and ordered the McClures to turn down the noise or they would confiscate their television and stereo system.

They did so, reluctantly, and when the police left, half-hour later, the noise started up again.

Jake wrote in his pad that Justin arrived home every day at 7 pm. No one cared or gave a shit if he was there or not, the mother was always half-dressed with the latest baby hanging off her tit. No one would notice if Justin disappeared. *Bonus,* Jake thought.

Justin left the house at 8 pm and headed in the direction of the old abandoned quarry. Jake followed and kept his distance. Justin met up with a girl, he recognised her as Lucy Ellis from school. They were in the same year. "Who would have thought of it?" Jake said under his breath. "Crocapigs." Then giggled to himself. Justin held her close and they walked hand in hand to the quarry.

Jake still kept his distance, watching them making out. Justin had his hand up her skirt, she was groaning with pleasure as she kissed him. Justin pulled down his trackies and they started having sex. Jake took out his writing pad and wrote Lucy's name next to Justin's. Jake took no pleasure in watching them, however, seeing them together brought bile up into his mouth. Jake's watch pinged; it was 9 pm, he had to get home so he called it a night, realising he wasn't going to get anymore intel tonight. So he made his way home through the cornfield which came out at the bottom of steep hill.

Jake followed Justin over the week taking notes; he met up with the gang every day after school. All together, they headed to the local sweetshop; whilst one of them distracted the shopkeeper, the others stole sweets and pop. Once they had eaten their sweets, they hung out around the park until they were bored. Then they ripped number plates off cars and played knock down ginger on old folk's doors or threw eggs. If they saw a kid out all alone they would beat them up and steal everything they had on their person.

Justin would leave the group around 6:45 pm and headed home for 7 pm, then met up with Lucy just after 8 pm.

***

George Bradshaw was a little weasel; he never took the blame for anything, and it was always someone else that got the thick ear. Even at school, he would start the trouble, then take a step back and watched it all kick off. He was an average student, his home life was pretty normal, there was nothing unusual. He lived at 33 Sycamore Street. His father was a painter and decorator, his mother a nurse. He was the eldest of four siblings.

The family home was neat and tidy. They had a live-in au pair; she was about nineteen, slim, fit and attractive. She took on a share of the family's responsibility for childcare during the day and housework; she didn't live in the family home, but above the garage. On first impressions this seemed odd to Jake, there was nothing in George's life to explain his behaviour and treatment towards others and the attack on Ella.

Over the coming days, nothing was really happening. He took out his writing pad and wrote down the comings and goings of the household. The au pair was pretty much there all the time. The mother worked from 8 am to 8 pm. The father worked 8 am to 5 pm; however, he didn't take over the family responsibilities from the *au pair* when he came home. He said hello to the kids, interacted with them for a little while, and then watched TV with a beer.

George arrived home just after 7 pm, his younger siblings started going to bed at ten-minute intervals between one another. George sat and watched television with his dad for about twenty minutes until the au pair sorted out the younger kids. Then George went to his room.

The blinds in the living room were turned down slightly, so Jake could still see. As the au pair approached the father, he undid his zipper and she stripped naked, not like she had much on anyway. She bent down between his legs and sucked him off, fingering herself at the same time, whilst the dad sat back relaxed on the sofa. She then climbed aboard, straddled and rode him whilst he sucked her small breasts.

The session really didn't last that long. After it was over, they both hungrily kissed, then she got off him, got dressed and went to the kitchen and saw to dinner. Within ten minutes the wife came home from work. She kissed her husband, said hello to the *au pair* then went upstairs to see the kids and kissed them goodnight.

She changed into her pyjamas, then husband and wife excused the *au pair* and they sat down for dinner together. The *au pair* just went back to her room over the garage.

Jake was convinced that George must have known about his dad and the *au pair*. He wrote arsehole on his writing pad next to George's name and then went home. Over the coming days, Jake was convinced that George was a bored kid with an arsehole attitude, with nothing to do other than to cause trouble. He had very little interaction with his parents and siblings.

***

Heather Cilliërs was the newest member of the gang, only just moved to the area from South Africa. She was of mixed race but she didn't like that terminology as it made her feel like she was colourless, but instead referred to herself as multiracial. Her mother was French and her father was South African with some Irish thrown into the mix; her hair was braided and shaped into a shoulder length bob. She had big brown eyes with a beautiful smile. She was quite tall for her age and slender. She talked a lot, played the saxophone and is fluent in French.

Jake couldn't understand why she was hanging around with this crowd and it baffled him a great deal. This girl was bright, full of potential and pleasant. He was confused as to where she fit in with this group, but despite how impressed he was with this girl, he was not willing to show her any mercy. Jake took out his writing pad and next to her name wrote and said out loud, "Shame."

She lived at 22 Willow Crescent, the more upmarket side of town, her father was a professor of math. Her mother worked at the local newspaper selling advertising space. She had two elder brothers, both at university, one studying to be a solicitor and the other studying economics.

Heather would arrive home after school every day at 5 pm; she would then sit down with her parents and have dinner. After dinner, she would then go to her tree house for about half hour, then study for another half hour. Sometimes she went to No 16 where Peter Burns lived and stayed there for up to an hour, then came home.

There was lots of fun and laughter in this house. It was full of life and music, and at times, Jake found himself giggling. This girl was loved and she was wanted!

It was Friday and Jake was about to go home when he saw Natasha Cley and two other girls that he didn't recognise, walk round the top of the road. They knocked at Heather's door and waited. When Heather opened the door and reacted to seeing Natasha and her two friends, Jake was not ready for it and didn't expect it.

Heather stepped out onto the drive and shut the front door. There was an exchange with words, heated words, with Natasha poking Heather in the chest continuously until Heather passed her something. Jake couldn't quite make out what was handed over. The other two girls were goading Natasha, then she spat in Heather's face. All Jake heard as the three girls pushed past Heather elbowing her was, "We want double next week," then they turned and walked back the same way they came.

Now, Jake was really confused, these two girls were supposed to be friends, they hung around after school together, got into mischief together and there had been no sign that these two did not like each other. He knew this because he had been watching them for the past three weeks, so why would Natasha do this?

***

Kevin Stones was one nasty sonofabitch. He was tall, his hair was styled high and tight, just how the marines wore theirs. He was always wearing the latest designer fashions, and no one knew where he got the money from to buy this kind of designer clothing? He spent most of his time doing sports, mainly rugby and to be honest, he was really good and played for the school team. When he was not causing trouble, he drank canned lager and smoked cigarettes.

He was from a one-parent family; his father was in prison and was doing a seven-year stretch for fraud. The family lost everything. The house they were living in, belonged to his uncle on his mother's side. If it wasn't for his uncle they probably would have been homeless or living in some awful shelter.

His mother worked all hours on a production line, twelve-hour night shifts and any overtime that was available. Being the eldest of two, his younger sister Molly of seven years was part Down syndrome, and needed care. Whilst his mother was at work, he would always take care of Molly and made sure he was at home for 7 pm on the dot in readiness for when his mum went off to work.

Molly was the only person in the world he was nice to; he absolutely adored her and would do anything for her. If anyone made a spiteful comment or made fun of her, no matter who it was, they would feel the full force of his rage. When they first moved to 22 Westcolt Street after his father went to prison, people constantly stared and whispered. Over time, that had now subsided.

His mum went to work, and within fifteen minutes Natasha turned up at the door by herself. She stayed for about half hour then left. Around 9 pm two men, probably around the mid to late twenties, knocked at the door. They arrived holding no bags or containers, when they left within twenty minutes, they were holding a medium sized sports bag. Jake had an idea of what was in the sports bag, which urged him to want to know more about Kevin Stones and his activities.

The same two men arrived at the house once a week, same time and day every week. No one else was at the house when Kevin greeted the two men; his younger sister was always in bed. Jake scouted around the back of the house. He noticed a massive tree near the back of the house. He climbed the tree and sat there and watched. The tree gave him the perfect camouflage and cover. It wasn't dense enough for him not to see the back of the house but it had enough coverage for him not to be seen. There was a good size shed in the back garden that sat next to a Wendy house made from wood, with a climbing frame, slide and swing. The fence surrounding the garden was only three foot in height with a gate centrally positioned. The garden was a good size and was well kept; there was no sign of dogs or any other pets.

Jake found the tree uncomfortable to begin with and kept fidgeting until he found the perfect nook and settled into it. He must have been up that tree for about an hour and a half when he noticed Kevin walking out of the back door and into the shed with these two guys. They were again about fifteen to twenty minutes in the shed before they emerged with a sports bag and then left. Jake knew he had to see what was in the shed but he couldn't do it tonight, so he thought, he would leave it till weekend when he had more time.

The next couple of days zoomed by and Saturday soon arrived. Jake got up early and left the house and made his way to Kevin Stones' house. He watched the front of the house for a while, the mum left with little Molly in tow. She put her in the back of the car and then placed plastic baskets in the boot. Jake thought to himself, she is off food shopping, which means she will be out of the house for a couple of hours minimum, but there was no sign of Kevin.

Jake watched them drive away, then left it for fifteen minutes, then decided to walk casually around the back of the house, climb the tree and watch the back of the house for any movement or sign of life; he waited for a further half hour then decided to approach the garden.

The bolt on the gate was stiff and wasn't budging so Jake decided to climb over the gate which was quite sturdy. He approached the shed door which had a padlock, locking the door. He tried to look through the holes in the wood to see inside but it was too dark and the window on the side of the shed was whitewashed. "Fuck," he said to himself. Jake didn't hear the backdoor open but a flicker of sun light reflected off the back door and into his left eye. He slightly turned and saw

Kevin fastly approaching him with a baseball bat in his right hand.

Jake quickly turned and bolted, jumping the fence then ran down the alleyway onto Westcolt Street. He heard Kevin shout, "You fucker, I'll get you." Jake ran past Kevin's house, seeing Kevin from his left eye exiting his front garden and now hot on Jake's heels, still holding the baseball bat. Jake turned and ran onto St Giles Road and past Justin McClure's home. Kevin was still shouting out, "I'm gonna get ya, motherfucker," he then threw the baseball bat which hit Jake in the middle of his spine, then fell to the side of the road. It knocked Jake a little bit off course nearly losing his footing but he managed to stay upright and carried on running down St Giles Road with Kevin still hot on his heels.

Jake saw the cornfield up ahead and managed to find extra energy to keep on running. He could hear Kevin starting to fatigue but still managing to keep up. Jake jumped into the corn crop and quickly darted to the right, whilst Kevin continued forward, tripped, and fell onto his front, head first into the corn crop. Jake quickly reacted by kicking Kevin in the bollocks, the sound of Kevin screaming went straight through Jakes body with a feeling of satisfaction and exhilaration; red mist took hold of him.

He jumped onto his back digging his knees into Kevin's ribs, then grabbed his hair and the back of his head and forced it into the soil. Kevin, coughing and spitting, thrashed his arms and legs around and tried to move his body like a bucking bronco; Jake let go of Kevin's head and grabbed his right arm, with Kevin shouting obscenities and threats, Jake bent Kevin's arm up his back until he heard a loud crack and a sudden jolting movement of the joint as Kevin's shoulder dislocated. An almighty scream came out of Kevin and with Jake laughing, he started to punch and kept punching Kevin in the side of his head and face.

Kevin's body went limp and then slumped unconsciously underneath him. Jake's breathing was heavy, he felt excitement with shivers going up and down his spine. He got off Kevin and stood over him. He said in a low gravelled voice, "Yeah, you really got me didn't you, cunt!"

Jake didn't go back to Kevin's house after that so he laid low instead. He wasn't sure if Kevin recognised him but got angry and chastised himself with ten lashings of his belt down his back for being too cocky and eager. Kevin was found by the farmer, who called an ambulance and then Kevin's mother; he then spent a couple of days in a hospital for observation with his arm in a sling.

His mother had to take time off work. He was interviewed by the police and made up a cock and bull story which they accepted, not because they believed him but because it was too much time, effort and paperwork for anything else, so they just took a statement and left it at that.

***

Wilf Macintosh was a foster kid; this was his second family and he had been with them for nearly three years and so far, going okay. His maternal mother was murdered by his paternal father who injected her with heroin because she was going to leave and testify against him for the murder of an undercover police officer Michael Bray; Wilf was only two. His paternal father was serving sixty-two years for both murders and other crimes. He was deemed a risk to public safety and was beyond rehabilitation and placed in a maximum-security prison.

His grandparents on his mother's side took on parental responsibility, but that was cut short and within three years they died from a car accident whilst travelling in Italy. Wilf was being looked after by friends at the time. His paternal father was then approached in prison; as he had no family to speak of, he signed the boy over to the state care system.

Wilf was placed almost immediately with his first foster family and stayed with them just over four years. The first six months were going okay, and he settled in well with the other three foster kids. They were all like little soldiers and didn't speak much to each other. It was the little things at first, with not drying the plates properly, for that you got a poke and a tongue lashing, "Do it again," Mrs Currie would shout.

The kids didn't have time to play like other children outside the hours of school. From morning to night, they had constant chores in and outside of the house. Overtime, the pokes turned into slaps, and then the slaps turned into punches. Sometimes they would be whipped with a cane for no reason. The bruising, cuts and sores were missed or ignored by the school and Social Services.

Mr and Mrs Currie were pillars of the community. She worked part-time and he was a councillor. Everyone said they were brave taking in three foster kids. It was all for show; the only time the boys were allowed to behave like normal children was when they had company and that was not very often. Mr and Mrs Currie didn't have any children of their own; Mrs Currie could not conceive, they spent thousands on IVF and when that didn't work they paid for a surrogate, Mrs Currie was traumatised and bereft with grief when the baby was stillborn.

Over time, she became desperate, bitter and very sad. She turned to the Catholic Church for support and guidance. The church was on good terms with the care home and introduced Mr and Mrs Currie to the idea of fostering. They both agreed to take a stern harsh approach when it came to raising the boys; they didn't realise they took it too far and turned their punishment into cruelty.

One of the boys decided he had had enough and ran away. The police picked him up two and a half hours later. He showed and told the authorities of the cruelty and punishments and said he wouldn't go back. The police and Social Services opened up an investigation; they were shocked by what they discovered. The three boys were separated and placed back into the care system.

Wilf was again almost immediately placed with his second fostered family, Mr and Mrs Jameson and had been with them now for almost three years. He liked the Jamesons; again they had no children of their own. They were good people and didn't believe in punishments but rather a bohemian approach to parenting, you sat around the kitchen table and talked things through. There wasn't really any rules or boundaries, but three things Mr Jameson insisted on and that was that Wilf must attend school; dinner was at 5 pm and not to be missed, and he must be home for 9 pm.

After school was his time and at weekends they would do family stuff together like going to parks, cycling, hiking, museums and anything that had a historical interest, they would go and see. Wilf, however, was bored most of the time when going to these places of interest but he indulged them.

Jake monitored him over the week and discovered that Wilf and Heather were becoming close. When the others were out of sight they would hold hands down the street, on the way to Heather's house but would take the longer route. Wilf then pecked her on the cheek before heading home himself.

Wilf and Heather both met up again after 6 pm to 8:30 pm, both walking hand in hand along the canal, talking and laughing; the rest of the gang were nowhere to be seen.

***

Natasha Cley was a really pretty girl; pot doll looks with long blonde hair and a slim frame. The boys drooled over her and the girls hated her, not because of the way she looked but because she was a horrible person. This was her third school, expelled from two private schools for bullying and violence towards other pupils, there was also a rumour of a sexual relationship with the maths teacher, Mr Bone, but that was just a rumour. Due to her appalling reputation no other private school would take her, no matter how much money her parents offered them. She had no other option but to be enrolled into the local comprehensive school, where she felt superior to everyone else.

Both of her parents were solicitors and financially comfortable. They were at the top of their profession, both senior partners. They lived at Cathedral View, which used to be an old barn and sat on ten-acres, now converted into a four bedroom with indoor swimming pool and library. She had her own walk-in wardrobe and bathroom. She was the second of three girls. Her sisters, Felicity and Penelope, equally attractive, would tease her and pull her hair for being expelled and had to go to the local comprehensive.

She hated the teasing which made her feel insecure and depressed. She isolated herself from her family and would, most days, stay in her room when she was home. Her old friends wouldn't have anything to do with her and she wasn't invited to parties as now they considered her not one of them, which depressed her even more. The only enjoyment she had was riding her horse.

Kruger was a big horse with two-tone colouring of brown and black. He was a feisty fucker with a bad temperament; they both understood each other, he wouldn't let anyone else ride him, and he was the only thing she cared about. They would ride for hours, she would muck out his stable, feed and groom him.

Natasha always acted like butter wouldn't melt when she was with her parents. Her sisters on the other hand, knew exactly what she was like and weren't fooled by her sneaky antics. To get her own back on her sisters, sometimes she would put cat litter or horse shit and smothered it into their bed linen. Her sisters would get their own back by sticking her head down the toilet into pee water then flushing it.

Her father was always shouting at the three of them, sometimes he would have to walk out of the house because they drove him to distraction with the way they treated one another. Felicity and Penelope disliked Natasha with a passion. What their parents saw was Felicity and Penelope ganging up and bullying Natasha, they never wanted to see the other side of her, the really nasty horrible self-indulged, self-absorbed fucking bitch that she was. To them, she was the apple of their eyes and got anything she asked for.

Natasha treated people like shit, other than her parents, grandparents, or anyone she felt she had use for or could benefit her in some way. She was the school bully and anyone who had been on the receiving end of her temper avoided her like the plague. She could fight and it was real nasty when she got hold of you. The only person she would never cross was Kevin. He didn't only scare her but he excited her as well.

Jake knew there was no point in monitoring Natasha, he watched her and made notes whilst she was with the gang and he knew and already made up his mind on the outcome of this gang. All he had to do now was to physically prepare and figure out how he would lure this group into the woods.

Chapter 13

Matthew was beside himself, and had been for weeks. He couldn't talk to anyone, he bottled up his feelings and the knock-on effect to that was lashing out at everyone including his friends. Even his teachers noticed the change in him and tried to talk to him, but he wouldn't say anything to anyone. His mum tried to talk to him but all he could do was to ignore and not look at her; after all the problem stemmed from her.

He loved his mum and he knew if he said anything, all hell would break loose. God knows what would happen if his dad ever found out. He grew up seeing his dad beat his mum over nothing but mostly over Jake. He thought things would get better when Jake left to go and live with their grandparents, and it did for a while, lasted for about six weeks.

There was no doubt that his dad loved his mum; well, he certainly gave that impression. It was the attack that changed everything, the drinking came not long after that and the late nights at the pub. His dad was a hard worker and farming was hard, dealing with livestock, crops and drought. He had so many skills under his belt from horticulture to metal and woodwork, there was nothing he couldn't do. He was a really skilled man, a jack-of-all-trades. Matthew loved the farm and wanted to be a farmer just like his dad. He looked up to and admired him.

As soon as he got home from school, he did his homework and chores around the house and farm; then he was out in the field helping his dad. When his dad wasn't drinking he was the best dad in the world. They had fun with lots of banter and messing around. That was a good day!

Sometimes Mark and Henry would tag along but that was when nothing would get done. Knowing they hadn't done their chores around the farm, Matthew would head back earlier and quickly do it for them. Not because he wanted to, he had other things to be getting on with, but he figured if Dad was happy and not shouting and being angry all the time, then Mum, and them would be having a really good day as well.

Once John finished ploughing the fields, he and Matthew sat down under the tree, drank water and talked. "So, what's been going on with you, these last few weeks, you haven't been yourself?"

"Nothing is wrong with me."

"That's not what I asked."

"I mean nothing is going on."

"You know what I want, and you know I will get it, so c'mon start talking," said John, looking at Matthew.

"I'm being bullied at school by three older boys," Matthew said looking out into the distance, trying not to look directly at his dad.

"Bullshit," taking another swig of water.

"What!" Matthew said, surprisingly looking at his dad

"That's not what's going on. I taught you to fight, remember. We are not leaving this spot till you tell me."

"I told you nothing is going on," raising his voice as he started to feel uneasy, knowing no matter what he said, he wasn't leaving from under this tree without telling him.

"You say that one more time, I bloody dare you. Start talking!" he said sternly.

"I saw and heard them," Matthew said in a whisper.

"Who?"

"Mum and Doctor Moody, the night you came home drunk and parked your truck in the tree."

"What were they doing?"

Matthew hunched his shoulders and wished the ground would open up a swallow him up whole.

"I won't ask again Matthew!" directly looking at him.

"They were kissing and holding each other and saying the L word."

"And, where was I?"

"You were passed out on the sofa. Mum and me, got you into the house from the car, then she called Dr Moody. He came over and checked you out. Then I was sent back to bed, but I didn't go back to bed. I sat on the top step of the stairs and saw them in the kitchen. They were talking, and Doctor Moody was telling her that he missed and loved her. They were kissing and holding each other."

"I take it, you haven't spoken to your mum about what you have seen."

"No, I can't look at her, Dad."

"It's okay. I already know Matthew, your mum already told me. You're a little bit confused with the details, you should have said something sooner, instead of bottling everything up," said John placing his hand onto Matthews shoulder and giving it a squeeze for reassurance whilst at the same time the rage inside of him boiling up like a volcano. Matthew turned tearfully towards his dad then they both hugged. "Dry your tears, wash your face and head back to the house. I'll be along in a minute," said John. Matthew nodded, feeling better, but also stupid, but the weight on his shoulders disappeared.

John waited for Matthew to be out of sight before he started to punch and kick the side of the truck, cursing Faith with every breath. "Bitch, whore, slag, you lying fucking cunt," he said out loud with tears streaming down his face. Holding his stomach, his guts retching so much he vomited in front of the truck. The love he had for her was now gone and hatred took its place.

Later that evening, the boys were in bed, asleep and Faith was crashed in bed after having a bath from a long and strenuous day. John stood in the doorway of their bedroom just looking at her. The bed sheets curved around the silhouette of her naked body. His cock went hard; slipping out of his clothing, he slid in around her.

Taking the KY Jelly from the top drawer of the bedside cabinet, he started to massage the jelly into her anus. Faith stirred and moved in rhythm to his fingers inside of her. John smothered his thick hard throbbing cock with KY then slid his penis into her anus. Alternating his cock between the anus and pussy, he was still wrapped around her on his side. He lifted her leg over his, exposing her pussy, he placed his thumb onto her clit and started to work it, whilst his finger pumped her soaking wet juicy pussy.

Bringing his mouth down close to her ear, his other arm wrapped around her, his hand squeezing her breast and tweaking her nipple. His soaking wet fingers turned into a fist, whilst his thumb was still working her clit, with his cock pumping deep inside of her. His fist slipped into her pussy and he pumped deep inside of her. Her pleasure was short lived; placing his lips close to her ear, he whispered, "I know about you and Mitch Moody, cunt." Her eyes flung open wide and she tried to break free but was unable to move; she was pinned to him.

He clasped her ear with his teeth, as he bit down hard, the blood from her ear filled his mouth. Hysterically pleading with John to stop, removing his fist from her fanny, his hand grabbed her hair and pushed her head into the pillow, she tried to wrestle herself free but couldn't as he was too strong and pinned her down.

Moving his body, keeping hold of her hair, he turned her, so she was face down. Parting her bum cheeks, he thrust himself back inside of her. He could hear the pain in her voice as she cried out for him to stop but the more she whined, the harder and deeper he plunged inside of her anus, until spilling his seed. "That was the best ever, babe."

He shoved her away from him, falling hard on her side with a thud onto the floor. He left the bedroom whistling and got into the shower leaving her, lying on the floor sobbing and shaking.

Chapter 14

John drank himself stupid at his local pub, 'The Jolly Whistler'. Tina was a barmaid and had worked there for a few years now; over time she had gotten to know John. She was a dyed blonde, medium built, with full breasts and an arse to die for. The men drooled over her as she served them; she wasn't particularly attractive, but the body made up for that. With no husband on the scene, she had a daughter of sixteen, named Chloe.

Her advances towards John were never reciprocated. He would never have cheated on Faith till now, and the thought never even crossed his mind. The arguments between him and Faith became exhausting, she nit-picked and nagged about his drinking, then the amount he drank and then it escalated from that to that fucking child, Jake. Her and the boys wanted to go see him and her parents, see how he is getting on, what's he been up to. John put his foot down at that point and told her they weren't going anywhere, and to shut her up and for her troubles, he gave her a slap.

Every time John beat Faith, an overwhelming feeling of guilt went through his body. He hated himself for it, he loved the bones of her, worshipped the ground she walked on, but she knew which buttons to push and by gum, she pushed them! She questioned everything and had to be argumentative about everything he said and did. She just couldn't take things as they were, always over analysing. Well, he was fed up, broken and felt suffocated.

John had a lot of guilt to deal with and a lot to answer for. He was the one who invited his old school buddy into their home; he hadn't seen Robin in ten years at that point. Robin joined the military, then they lost contact with each other. Then one day John walked into the pub and there sat Robin, he only came back because his father had died. With no place to stay, John offered Robin a room.

The first few days were grand and it was like old times. Faith was okay with Robin staying at first, then the complaining came, the moaning, the whining. John thought to himself he should have listened; he should have seen what was going on. Alarm bells should have sounded, but they didn't. He was just over the moon that his best pal had returned even if it was only for a little while.

It wasn't until that day, that dreadful day, when everything, his whole life went to shit. It was too late when John realised his best buddy was an animal. John walked in on them in the kitchen which looked like a bomb had hit it. Matthew, Henry and Mark were in the playpen that he made, all crying. Robin had Faith pinned to the floor, all battered and bruised, he could see her torn knickers, her top and skirt ripped. He had a knife held to her throat, raping her.

John couldn't believe what he was seeing, what he was hearing, when his senses came back to him he was about to smash a kitchen chair over Robin. "You do, she dies, I will cut her fucking throat!" pushing the knife deeper into her throat Faith gargled and groaned, she closed her eyes with tears streaming down her face. John was paralysed holding the chair in mid-air, he felt helpless as all he could do was watch his buddy raping his wife. When Robin finished they both fought and hard, with Robin getting the better of him and stabbing him in the shoulder, John fell back and banged his head against the kitchen cabinet.

Robin fled taking Mark with him. John managed to call the police and ambulance, not realising Mark was missing. He crawled up to Faith, hysterically kissing and touching her beautiful face, calling her name, desperately trying to get some kind of response from her. He heard sirens in the distance and then a screeching noise. When Robin fled with Mark, he left him in the middle of the road. Luckily the police officer who was driving was paying attention to the road, narrowly missing Mark, swerving into the verge.

John had to call his neighbour to come and take care of the boys whilst the paramedics stabilised Faith and saw to John's injuries, then sped them away at high speed. The police in hot pursuit of Robin, with dogs picking up his scent and trail, they followed him through the woods onto the fen road. They managed to pick him up two miles down the road trying to thumb a lift. They found the knife Robin threw away down by the creek, two hours after that.

The intensity of Faith's injuries had her laid up for weeks; as well as the cuts and bruising she had a broken jaw, a cut to her throat. Fortunately the knife was blunt and didn't penetrate too deeply, two cracked ribs, a fractured wrist, concussion, and she was pregnant; her parents came to stay and looked after them.

Faith was never well enough to testify in court so she had to be linked in via camera. Robin was sent to military prison for going AWOL and assault and battery on a fellow colleague, then from there he would be sent to a public prison to carry out the rest of his sentence of fifteen years.

Since that day John was a haunted man, a changed man, a rejected man.

Chapter 15

Tina comforted John during her twenty-minute break; he was pissed didn't know what he was saying or doing and found himself the next morning waking up next to her. "Ah, shit," John said under his breath. Quietly sneaking out of the bedroom with his clothes, he dressed, left a note for Tina saying, "Sorry, had to go, speak to you soon," then headed for home.

Arriving at the farm, he saw that Faith was already up and about; the boys were still in bed. Standing in the doorway of the kitchen, Faith turned and looked at him, "Coffee?"

"Yes, please," as he sat down. Faith turned and sat down with the coffees.

"Where have you been?" looking at him with all the hatred in the world.

"Pub."

"What, all night?"

"No, woke up next to Tina," saying that with a smug look, wanting to see her reaction.

"Fucked her, then?"

"Don't know, don't remember; woke up naked, she was also naked so I suppose, yes."

"Bastard," crossing her arms, giving him the dead eye.

"Oh, that's rich coming from you. Mitch Moody; when did that start?"

"Eighteen months after Jake was born. We were in a dark place, still are and I ended it over a year ago now, but we had sex a few weeks ago."

"Charming, a full blown affair all this time; I am a bloody fool," running his hand throw his hair.

71

"No. Not a full-blown affair. We got close; he attended to my injuries, initially from Robin and now he attends to my injuries from you."

"So what, am I supposed to be grateful?"

"No, just trying to be honest. How about you do the same. You knew Robin was a monster but you, you turned into my nightmare. That man tore us apart and you let him and you're still letting him. You blamed Jake and took your anger out on an innocent boy who knows nothing about what happened and you blamed me as well; that's why you drink, that's why you hurt me."

"That's not fair, that's really not fair, and I have never blamed you."

"Yes, you do. You think I caused that situation, that somehow it was my fault. You invited that bastard into our home. I told you, time and time again, the things he was doing, that he frightened me and you chose to ignore me."

"I thought you were being dramatic, reading into things that weren't there. You're always moaning and whining about something. When I was around, you seemed to get along fine, there was no indication, with no sign of what happened was going to happen."

"Dramatic, moaning, whining? Is that all you see?"

"No, you suffocate me Faith, I have always loved you, I have always been faithful, but you have broken me, I have never felt good enough for you, nothing is good enough for you and it's easier to always blame our troubles on that day," said John.

"John, that's not true. You treat me more badly than a beaten dog."

"You wanted to be honest, now let's be honest. Our marriage is over and I want you out, gone today."

"You what? What about the boys? I am their mum and they need me, you're the one that's leaving, John?"

"I think not. This is my house and my farm and the boys will stay here with me. Go to your parents, go and see Jake. Say goodbye to the boys and I want you gone. If you're here when I get back, I will throw you out!" with that, John gets up from the table and walked out of the house slamming the front door.

Faith stayed sitting and breaking down in tears. With her head in her hands, Matthew approached her and put his arms around her, squeezing her tight. They stayed like that for a while with Faith sobbing. "Matthew, please help me get your brothers dressed, quickly and quietly," said Faith as they both headed up the stairs.

Matthew quickly got dressed then went into Henry and Mark's room, woke them up and got them dressed. "Where are we going," said Henry. "We are going to see Nana and Gramps," said Matthew.

"Yeah," Mark and Henry cheered.

Whilst Matthew sorted out his brothers, Faith threw clothes into black bin bags and anything else she thought they would need, and then took them downstairs. She reversed the truck up to the front door and started to load the truck. She saw the tractor in the distance approaching. "Shit, boys hurry up," said Faith shouting up the stairs. "Why are you taking so long, boys hurry up?" said Faith, getting impatient. She ran upstairs only to find the boys were not up there. "What," she said to herself. She looked in all the upstairs rooms then headed back downstairs; they weren't in the kitchen either.

Starting to panic, "Boys, where are you?" as she turned into the living room, they were sitting on the sofa with John standing over them.

"What do you think you're doing!" said John.

Ignoring what he said, "Boys come on, let's go, get into the truck," said Faith, brushing past John. The boys were about to stand, "Sit down, you're not going anywhere," said John, clenching his fist.

With fear in her eyes and about to turn, John grabbed her by her neck and threw her against the wall. "I told you the boys are going nowhere, so what the fuck, do you think you are doing, taking my boys?"

"They are my boys, too," said Faith, shaking to the core.

"Not anymore they are not, now get out."

"No, not without my boys," with that she pushed herself from the wall, turned and pushed John off of her. Panting with every breath, she tried to pass him, heading towards the boys who were now scared and sobbing their little hearts out. John grabbed her arm and slapped her face; she slapped him back, hurting her hand in the process.

This time, he punched her in her face. She retaliated by slapping him again, then embedding her fingernails into his face, scratching downwards. He cried out in pain, grabbing her hair and then punched her in the stomach, winding her. She managed to catch her breath, and kneed him in the balls and ran into the kitchen. In pursuit of her, he grabbed her and threw her onto the kitchen table. They wrestled; she managed to grab hold of the ceramic fruit bowl that was in the centre of the table, spilling the contents onto the floor then smashed the bowl over John's head. "Fucking bitch," he shouted out, then kept slapping her in the face.

The boys, by this time, had moved into the corner of the living room, all huddled together scared and sobbing, with Matthew having his arms wrapped around them, trying with all his might to shield them from the screams from their mother, coming from the next room.

John grabbed hold of Faith by her hair, and pulled her off the table, she slumped onto the floor. He then started dragging her towards the front door and threw her out of the house. She darted for the truck but John got there first, and then removed the keys from the ignition. They fought for the keys, then John pushed her up against the car, and said, "Fuck off, you whore!" Faith spit blood in his face.

"I hate you, I fucking hate you," she screamed. He threw her to the ground, and kicked dirt at her. "Fuck off and don't come back!" Faith managed to stand shaking, walking away weeping with convulsive gasps, leaving her boys behind. She kept looking back as she walked down the drive. Seeing John standing there watching her as she walked away.

Matthew knew where the mobile phone was hidden that Dr Moody gave his mum. Henry, Mark and him took the bins bags back upstairs and put their clothing and stuff back in their closets. He could hear his dad downstairs pacing. Matthew went into his parents' bedroom to retrieve the mobile phone from under the carpet in the closet and quietly phoned Dr Moody.

Chapter 16

It would take another three weeks for Jake to put his plan into action. He attended school as normal and didn't start to put his plan into action until after lunch. When he saw any of them he would shoulder nudge them when passing. To really get their attention, Jake walked up to Kevin, "Would you like me to run away so you could see the back of my head and then maybe let you catch me this time?"

"You what?"

"You heard, dick head. Did you enjoy eating dirt?"

"BASTARD, you're dead, you're so dead!" said Kevin with pure anger on his face.

"Hey Kevin, there's a tree with a noose that has your mong sister's name all over it," said Jake, giving Kevin the bird as he walked away.

Kevin launched himself at Jake but was stopped by Natasha and Wilf. "Not here dude, too many spectators, after school we will get him, all of us!" said Wilf, in his ear.

"Jake, what have you done, they won't stop till they get hold of you," said Ella, scared and concerned. Jake held her face in his hands and said, "I'm gonna get them, all of them for what they did to you. I won't let them hurt you again."

"Jake, they haven't come near me since the attack."

"They will, they are just biding their time, and then they will come for you like they do with the others. Trust me Ella. Don't wait for me after school, go straight home," said Jake as they headed to English Class.

The bell rang at precisely 3:15 pm, Ella went straight home and Jake went to his locker, changed his clothing to his tracksuit and placed his school clothing in his rucksack then left the building by the back door.

He ran at a steady pace across the playing field. "There he is, get him," said the six. Jake got to the perimeter fence and hauled himself over it, looking back through the fence seeing the six running towards him, catching his breath, he smiled and chuckled to himself. Waiting for them to get closer before he headed into the woods, so they knew where he is heading and can follow.

"I think that's close enough," he said to himself and started running again, keeping a comfortable distance. Running into the woods, he climbed the tree he had already chosen, lots of foliage and cover, enough not to be seen. He put on his gloves and balaclava, leaving his rucksack on a branch up the tree. There were four dirt paths he could see going in different directions. He could hear the group fast approaching. Once entering the woods, they stopped to catch their breaths. "He could be anywhere," said Heather.

"Right, let's split, four paths, choose one. When you catch him, shout," said Kevin.

Kevin and Wilf chose to go alone whilst the rest paired off, Justin and Heather together and Natasha and George together. Jake made a mental note of who went where. He decided to take out Justin and Heather first as they were the weakest link out of the gang.

Climbing down from the tree he took the direction of Justin and Heather; it wasn't long until he stumbled across them as they were sitting on a fallen tree looking bored. Jake saw a branch on the floor and walked forward so it snapped and made a cracking noise. Both Justin and Heather looked up and in the direction of the noise and they saw Jake; they jumped down from the tree and chased him.

Jake ran in the direction of his markers and past them. Heather was faster than Justin, and it wasn't long until they were separated. Heather left Justin behind but was close enough for Justin to see which direction they were heading in. Jake lured Heather in the direction of her tree. He stopped and hid behind the nearest tree and saw her run past him.

He picked up a stone then whistled; she stopped and turned, looking around, but didn't see anything. Jake whistled again and let himself be seen by Heather. Stepping quickly towards her, his arm reaching back, he threw the stone hitting her on the side of her head which unbalanced her, throwing her to the ground. Jake quickly grabbed her and dragged her by her hair into the bushes, covering her mouth. He could hear Justin heavily breathing, calling out for Heather.

Heather drowsy, dizzy and disorientated, felt all her strength and energy was being drained from her body. She felt blood running down her temple. Jake still had his hand covering her mouth. He took out a handkerchief from his pocket and gagged her. She started crying, "Oh 'boohoo' you fucking bitch. Now move, through there," said Jake. Doing as he said, she moved. They walked one hundred and fifty metres through undergrowth.

They reached her tree; he pushed her up against the trunk and punched her in the stomach, doubling her up. She tried to cry out. Jake quickly dug up his tools, taping her hands around her back and then taping her ankles together. Jake then tied Heather to the tree with the rope and tied a binding knot. Jake then picked up the bungee, swinging it and struck her with the hooked end. Her screams were muffled. Jake smiled knowing she was in pain and it pleased him.

The more he struck her with the bungee, the more powerful he felt. He could hear her muffled pleas but he wasn't ready to show any mercy, not for any of them. He discarded the bungee and picked up the knife. He thrust the knife into her ribs and twisted, puncturing her lung. He could hear the air escaping from the hole. Watching her gasp for air, with tears running down her cheeks, he could see her starting to lose consciousness.

***

Justin was lost. He felt like he was going round in circles and Heather was nowhere to be seen. He called her constantly but there was no reply. The woods scared him, every noise made him jump. Jake was watching him from five meters away and couldn't help himself from treading on branches that cracked under his weight, just to see Justin jump out of his skin.

As light as he could, trying not to make a sound, Jake took a run towards Justin. As he approached the back of him, Jake lifted the stick and smashed it around his head. Justin fell to the ground sideways, screaming, just like a baby wailing. To shut him up he pulled out his large handkerchief, the same one he had used on Heather, and stuffed it into Justin's mouth, muffling his cries. Jake then tied Justin's hands behind his back and told him to get on his feet, walking through the undergrowth towards the tree Jake had picked for Justin.

Jake pushed Justin up against the tree. Justin pleaded with Jake to let him go and he wouldn't tell anyone. Jake punched Justin in his balls. In a matter of seconds, Justin was overcome by a crippling nausea; his knees met his chest with tears streaming down his face. Jake tied Justin to the tree, taping his ankles together, preventing Justin from kicking out.

Justin was unable to breathe with the handkerchief still stuffed in his mouth and with the punch in the bollocks, he sucked the handkerchief deeper down into his throat. He started to shake uncontrollably, his body thrashed about with sudden jerks like he was having a fit, his whole body convulsed. It took about four to six minutes for Justin to die. Jake took out his knife and thrust the knife into his ribs and twisted, puncturing his lung. He took a step back and watched him die.

***

It wasn't long for Jake to pick up the trail of George and Natasha; they were arguing, and with Natasha threatening him, George told her to "Fuck off", shoved her hand off him and then walked away in Jake's direction.

"Kevin will kill you if you stop looking, weasel," she shouted out putting her hands on her hips. She turned and walked deeper into the woods.

Jake knelt down, hiding himself in the undergrowth and watched George marched past him. He quietly followed him back to the woods opening. Jake took out his knife, jumped out of the bushes and stabbed George in the ribs, turning the knife. He grabbed the scruff of his neck, throwing George forward in the direction of his tree.

George, disorientated, held his ribs with his hand as though they were falling out, trying to balance but was unable to and kept falling forward. Dirt sprayed up in his face and into his mouth, making him cough and spit. Jake thought to himself, "This is taking way too long." He kicked George up the arse, then said, "Move. Move faster," and then kicked him again.

Finally reaching their destination, after a lot of dragging and kicking, with George practically unconscious, Jake went through the motions of taping up his hands and feet then tying him to the tree. He heard a rustling noise about ten feet away. He saw a mass of blonde hair sticking out from the top of the undergrowth. "Well, now," he thought to himself.

He slowly made his way over, picking up a stone. Then, all of a sudden, Natasha sprang up and out from under the undergrowth, holding a big stick and into Jake's direct line of sight. He threw the stone, but only hit her temple, not enough to unbalance her, but enough to open up a flesh wound. "Where's George? What have you done with him?" said Natasha.

Jake looked behind himself and pointed to a tree, "Over there."

"Where? I can't see him."

"Behind that tree, over there," he said, looking back.

Natasha walked slowly, crossing her feet, as she walked in the direction of where George was, swinging her stick every so often, with Jake in toe, keeping a distance. Natasha gasped bringing her hands up to her mouth, dropping her stick, as her eyes fell onto George.

"Well that was stupid," said Jake, then stuck the knife into her back; she screamed and fell to her knees. Her screams echoed through the woodland. Stopping Kevin and Wilf in their tracks, both turned and headed in the direction of the screams.

Smacking her on the side of the head with the back of his knife, he taped her hands behind her back grabbing her hair and pulling her in the direction of her tree. He could feel her hair coming away from her head as he yanked it; she was quite resistant and kept lashing out with her feet by trying to kick him. Jake grabbed her heel and lifted her leg, sending her backwards onto her back crashing into the ground.

Not far from her tree, he stabbed her in the thigh, twisting the knife. Her thigh bled out, and he knew she hadn't got long before she became unconscious. With all his strength, he dragged her to her final destination but he didn't tie her up, instead he cut her throat and stabbed her fourteen times throughout her body, then wrote 'BITCH' on her forehead.

Jake headed back to the tree, where he left his rucksack; he climbed the tree and took out a tuna and cucumber sandwich and ate it, washing it down with some water. Leaning back on the trunk, resting, he started thinking about his next move; the adrenaline was still rushing through his body with the feeling of invincibility. His plan was to leave Kevin until last; he saw him as a formidable opponent and will relish in his demise.

Still in the tree with his arm resting behind his head, Jake heard voices; it was Wilf and Kevin.

"Wilf."

"Kev."

They both said in unison. "Did you hear the screams?" said Wilf.

"Yes, but whose?"

"Have you seen any of the others?"

"No," said Kevin, shaking his head.

"I do not like this Kev."

"I don't either, nothing to see back there, no sign of that little fucker."

"I think we should get out of here?"

"Not without the others, and not until we have found that little bastard."

"Sod you, I'm going."

Wilf turned and was about to walk off when Kevin grabbed him by the scruff of his neck and pushed him up against the tree. "I said not until we find the others, okay," applying pressure, pushing Wilf into the tree. "Okay, okay," said Wilf taking in a deep sigh.

"We are going this way," said Kevin, walking in the direction of the dead four.

"Why that way, there is no path," shouted Wilf.

"Can't you see the undergrowth has been disturbed and broken in places," said Kevin, shaking his head in disbelief.

As Wilf and Kevin headed into the undergrowth, it was Jakes cue to climb down from the tree and follow them. Keeping the knife in his right hand, he moved quickly, gaining speed, and approaching Wilf. He whistled as Wilf turned his head looking back over his right shoulder, and sheer terror fell over his face, seeing only a knife flying through the air in his direction. Before he could react, the knife penetrated deep into his left eye. Feeling the cold steel slicing through his organ, it felt pretty surreal. At first it felt odd, a sharp, but not intense pain.

The stabbing was awful, he felt the life drain from his body. For what seemed like an age he was paralysed and in shock as the knife went in, turning his knees to jelly as his breath left his body. He remembered gasping whilst at the same time being surprised at the brilliant, intense feeling. Falling to the ground, still orientated and aware of his surroundings, seeing Jake standing over him, "Why?" said Wilf.

"Because of what you did to Ella."

"Ella, who is Ella?"

"What?" Jake said, as the penny dropped, which made him even madder. He grabbed Wilf's hair and pulled back his head. Pulling out the knife, he then slit his throat and then thought to himself *that made you smile*, then sniggered at his own comment.

Knowing that Kevin wasn't too far away, he headed deeper into the undergrowth. "I've seen your handy work,"

Kevin shouted out coming into view ten meters away. He removed his balaclava, so Kevin got to see his face before the last battle, the final confrontation.

Both boys came face to face, chests puffed out like a peacock. "All this for that scrawny bitch Ella? Must be love. I'll pay her a visit when I am finished with you," Kevin said with a smile, all cock sure, tormenting Jake. "Why don't you lose the knife and fight me like a man!"

Jake said nothing, just stood there, staring into Kevin's face. Jake dropped his knife from his right hand and before the knife hit the ground, Jake's left fist clenched and punched Kevin in the throat. Kevin took a few steps back, holding his throat and tried to breath. Looking up at Jake he took a run at him. Jake moved to the side and then brought down his elbow down onto the nape of the neck. Kevin fell to the ground, unconscious. Jake picked up his knife, grabbed Kevin's hair and pulled his head back. Kevin started to come around, looking up, seeing Jake smiling down at him, pure fear rushed over him. Jake slit his throat then, and watched the life drain out of Kevin.

His whole being was consumed with satisfaction, and an overwhelming feeling of invincibility, feeling like a god. His body was aroused with excitement, he felt his penis hardened, as he touched himself. Feeling the hardness of his length, he felt strange, his whole body tingled, there was a pulling in his lower abdomen, his breath became heavy and fast, he couldn't stop riding his shaft. He pulled down his trousers exposing his manhood, then wanked himself until spilling his seed into the soil.

Jake stood there a while, taking in the moment, breathing in the fresh air and listening to the chattering of birds echoing in his ears; he could hear the voices laughing on the breeze echoing through the woods. He closed his eyes and drank in the moment.

He went back to the tree to retrieve his rucksack, and then he went back to the bodies and the selected trees to remove all items that he had planted. He then cleaned up around the bodies removing all evidence and trace. Before leaving, he took a long hard look at each of his victims.

Chapter 17

Chief Inspector Peter Rankin was woken up in the early hours of Sunday 24th June on his mobile. "Okay, I'm on my way," he said, stretching and yawning as he forced himself out of bed, scratching his balls. Looking over his shoulder, he saw his wife Shirley stirring and turning over. He headed into the bathroom, he rinsed his face in cold water, looking in the mirror seeing strain and stress wrinkles all over his face, which aged him ten years, despite only just celebrating his forty-sixth birthday.

His dark coloured hair slightly turning grey and rugged looks, he was still an attractive man, he thought to himself, as he studied himself in the bathroom mirror. Though in reality he was a scrawny little runt with a face like a rat; he brushed his teeth, showered and got dressed. He kissed his wife on the forehead before leaving the bedroom and then looked in on his four-year-old son, Patrick, who was still asleep. He picked up his car keys and left the house.

Collecting coffee from the drive through, it took him another forty-five minutes before he reached the woodland. Senior Sergeant Simon Morgan was already on site. "Sir, we have six bodies, children, four boys and two girls. Sir, I have never seen," he said, distressfully shaking his head, trying to avoid vomiting.

"Are forensics on site?" said Chief Inspector Rankin.

"Yes, sir, the area is cordoned off and we are trying to contact the principal of the school as well," said Senior Sergeant Morgan.

"Sergeant, how were the bodies discovered?" said Chief Inspector Rankin.

"Dog walker, the dog ran into the undergrowth and when it was called to heel, the dog came back with a hand in its mouth. We have taken an initial statement and details," said Senior Sergeant Morgan.

"Thank you Sergeant. Point me in the direction of the Senior Forensic?" said Chief Inspector Rankin.

"You're going to need a handkerchief, sir, the air is rancid, it's not pretty in there, sir!" said Senior Sergeant Morgan.

"Thank you," said Chief Inspector Rankin.

As Chief Inspector Rankin approached and entered the cordoned area, he approached the Senior Forensic Investigator. "Hello I'm Chief Inspector Rankin. What can you tell me so far?"

"Hello Chief Inspector, I'm Molly Jenkins Senior Forensic," passing the Inspector a pair of latex gloves. "We have four boys and two girls. All with their throats cut and a puncture to the left lung with the exception of one victim, one of the girls, but we will come to that later on. I would say time of death, forty-eight hours. Would you like to see before we start removing the bodies?"

"Yes, yes, I think I will."

"It's not pretty; the wild pigs have been busy eating, cleaning up after the perpetrator and it's been raining as well. Here put these on over your shoes," she said.

"Are you always this direct?" he said.

"Sorry, yes, comes with the territory I'm afraid; prepare yourself, the stench will make you feel sick."

They both walked through the undergrowth to victim No 1, walking around the forensic team who were taking photos, samples and bagging evidence.

"Jesus!" he said putting the handkerchief to his face covering his mouth and nose. The smell in the air was vile, putrid, the state of the decomposing bodies brought up coffee and bile from the pit of his stomach. He could see the ripped, torn flesh, with some left on the ground, where the pigs had got disturbed and left it reluctantly.

"You can spit over there. I can see this is your first time; the pigs ate most of the arm, leaving the hand. We are lucky the pigs were disturbed."

"Lucky!" he said interrupting and retching at the same time.

"Yes Inspector, lucky. Otherwise there wouldn't be anything left to identify. You see, pigs will eat anything and everything including bone," said Molly.

"Why are some of the victims tied to trees?" he said

"If you look closer at the trunks, Inspector, you will see letters carved into the bark. I am guessing it's the victim's initials as all the trees have different letters. Also the positioning of the trees selected with its victim forms a circle. There is something else you need to see, Inspector. Look at the base of the tree; you will see the soil disturbed. It's the same for all the trees that were victim selected," said Molly.

"Oh my god, this was planned. Were there any instruments found, the murder weapon?" he said, scratching his fingers into his chin.

"No, he was very thorough with the clean-up. There's more, come with me, Inspector," said Molly.

They walked around to victim No 4, "Female, blonde, word 'BITCH' spelt in blood on her forehead and also stabbed multiple times and gutted; the others weren't killed like her. The perpetrator relished in this killing, it's vicious, vehement and he wanted her punished to make an example of her," said Molly.

"The killer definitely has made a statement. This is personal, a grudge, but who would kill six kids," said Chief Inspector Rankin running his hands through his hair.

"Definitely male, strong and intelligent," said Molly.

"Thank you Molly, keep me updated. I will leave Sergeant Morgan with you, if you need to get hold of me," said Chief Inspector Rankin. He was relieved to be getting out of there, as he started to make his way out of the woodland.

***

Senior Sergeant Morgan was nicknamed wanker by his colleagues. Not a well-liked member of the police force, especially amongst his female counterparts, he had been caught on a few occasions taking photos of female officers and wanking over them in the male toilets or changing rooms. Now, on his last formal warning and undergoing therapy, which was a decision his superiors made on the proviso that if he didn't go to therapy then his discharge from the force would be imminent, he was on his best behaviour, despite his urges for sexual pleasure.

His ex-wife, Wendy, left and divorced him because of the stigma and embarrassment he brought upon the family, she became paranoid over the events and believed she was mocked behind her back and felt she couldn't go out of the house without people staring and sniggering, even though none of the events were revealed to the public. So she decided to move to Melbourne with the three kids who now saw him rarely and now called someone else Daddy, which grated on him immensely.

Seeing Chief Inspector Rankin emerge from the woods, he started to head towards him. "Sir, we have managed to get hold of the school principal. She has closed the school for the next couple of days until we clear the area. Here is her number, sir; she would like you to contact her. Also the media have gotten wind and are arriving; the whole surrounding area is now cordoned off, and a journalist was seen and found in the woods taking photos," he said.

"What photos did they manage to take?" said the inspector.

"Hopefully, we caught them before they could get close enough, however, we have confiscated their equipment. I have the boys checking that out now before we hand it back. They are threatening us with law suits up the yin yang," said Sergeant Morgan.

"Good, zero tolerance, Sergeant Morgan. Before I head back to the station I will go and speak to the press. You have my number, Sergeant, anything further materialises, let me know straight away, and let me know if they find anything on their equipment," said Inspector Rankin

"Yes, sir," Sergeant Morgan replied.

Standing in front of the media Chief Inspector Rankin, looked comfortable and enjoyed the attention despite the terrible scenes he just saw. He then got into his car and headed back to the station.

Upon arriving at the station the press were waiting outside.

"Sir, the chief super is asking for an audience with you, as soon as possible," said Senior Sergeant Melody.

"Yes, thank you, Sergeant. That's where I am heading now. Could you check the logs from the last 48 hours on any reported missing children and put the list on my desk?" said Inspection Rankin, looking all rushed and flustered.

"Yes, sir," said Senior Sergeant Melody.

As he approached the chief's office, he said hello to his secretary, as she told him to go straight through, "He is waiting for you." He tapped on the door to gather his composure and then walked in. "Sir," he said, not noticing at first, the commander sitting in a chair. They exchanged pleasantries.

"Sirs, we have six dead children, brutally murdered in the Woodland Reserve located at the back of Rosemary Connolly Academy in the Northern Territory. Forensics estimate time of death within the last 48 hours. Area and surrounding, including the school have been cordoned off. The press are onsite and have already been caught within the restricted area and we have confiscated their equipment, only a matter of time until we know if they have contaminated the scene.

"Sir, I would like to be tasked with this one, I feel I am the right person for the job, to get a quick resolution," said Chief Inspector Rankin.

"We appreciate you putting yourself forward Chief Inspector, however, we feel this task will be better suited under someone with experience. Also, the individual we have in mind worked within Serious Crime at the London Metropolitan Police as a Detective and is highly specialised within this field and we are very lucky to have her, Chief Inspector Suzanne Jenson," said the commissioner.

"Inspector Rankin, we want the both of you to work together on this but Chief Inspector Jenson will take the lead," said the chief super.

Hearing her name, made him cringe inside. If memory served him correctly, she was extremely attractive, long brunette hair, slim, fit and very sexy. His advancements towards her came to nothing. She was a sergeant back then and didn't play like the other females.

"Yes, sirs. When we will be expecting her?" he replied.

"She is already en route, so probably the next two to three hours," said the Chief Super. He tried to hide the dread that appeared all over his face. "I take it there isn't going to be any problems or issues, Chief Inspector Rankin?" the Chief Super asked directly, staring at him.

"No, sir, no issues or problems," said Chief Inspector Rankin.

"Very well, you have a lot to do. We will let you get on, and I want daily reporting chief inspector and nothing is released to the press unless I specifically approve it," said the Chief Super, with the Commissioner nodding like a lapdog.

With that Chief Inspector Rankin left the office deflated, his ego just clinging on to the soles of his feet. He headed to the male toilets and washed his face. Looking in the mirror, he said to himself, "C'mon Peter, pull yourself together. It's been ten years." He took a pee and washed his hands, then headed back to his office.

When he opened the door, a second desk and computer had already been delivered. *Great*, he thought. His office was big enough to fit two more desks but he liked the space and now it has been invaded. A coffee machine was another new addition to his office. He turned around scratching his head, growling under his breath.

***

Suzanne Jenson arrived at the station at approximately 3:45 pm. She was in uniform, her hair pulled back into a bun. She wore no makeup; her nails were freshly manicured which showed off her sparkling engagement ring. The reaction was always the same when she arrived at a new station; the men couldn't do enough to help her and gave her all the attention in the world. The women, on the other hand, weren't as forthcoming and it always took a while for them to become friendly.

"Can I help you, ma'am?" said the Sergeant on the desk.

"Yes, I am Chief Inspector Jenson; the chief super is expecting me," she replied.

"We have been expecting you, ma'am, if you can sign the register and I will get someone to escort you," said the sergeant.

"Thank you," she replied.

Making her way up to the chief super's office, memorising the layout as she went. The building was relatively new, completed three years ago and with a gymnasium and cafeteria which looked out onto its own green space and was fully enclosed, which pleased her. The super's office was situated on the fourth floor. She was impressed with how modern it looked. She could have taken the lift, but wanted to walk and to get to the layout and know her way around.

On reaching the super's office, she said hello to his secretary. "He is waiting for you, go straight in," she said with a smile.

"Thank you," replied Inspection Jenson.

Inspector Jenson tapped on the door and entered.

"Suzanne, how the devil are you?" said the chief super getting up from his desk, making his way over to her.

"Hello Simon, yes, it's been a while, how is the family? How is Kate?" she said, with a beaming smile.

"Fine, all is fine and dandy. We have just celebrated our twenty-seventh wedding anniversary in Alaska, of all places, it was her idea she wanted to go somewhere cold," he said, rolling his eyes with a little chuckle.

"Well, she definitely got what she wanted and congratulations I am really chuffed for you both," she replied.

"Come, come sit down. Coffee is already waiting for you and I take it you are still partial for the old Ginger Nut. See I remembered," he said.

"Did you really remember or was it Kate that reminded you? Spill, 'cos you know I will ask her," she said, all comical.

"Okay, I surrender, it was Kate, but let's talk shop. I am sorry to get in touch with you under these terrible circumstances. However, we need someone with your experience and expertise on this," he said, sipping his coffee.

"What do you have for me? I hear from the news on the radio that a body has been found in woodland," she said.

"Six children to be precise," he said

"Six? Did you say six children? Oh my God, Simon!" she said, totally shocked, bringing her hands to her face.

"You will also be working alongside Inspector Rankin but you have overall jurisdiction and control, we have put you in the same office as him, as well," he said. Seeing her reaction sent a cold chill up through his body, seeing she wasn't happy.

"I take it he is aware I am coming on board?" she said.

"Yes, and I saw him grimace; any problems, you come straight to me, ok," he said.

"Ok," she replied finishing her coffee.

***

She made her way down to the third floor, again, walking and taking the stairs rather than the lift. She finally arrived at what would be her office for the next coming months. Peter sat at his desk typing away. "Hello Peter," she said, with a smile walking over to her desk.

"Hello Suzanne," he replied, sitting back in his chair folding his hands behind his head.

She could feel his eyes on her, watching her every move, which made her cringe. *Come on girl, pull yourself together, you can do this,* she thought to herself as she settled at her desk.

"Listen Suzanne, can we clear the air? We have to work with each other on this case and I would rather do this as friendly colleagues rather than enemies. Would you like a coffee?"

"Yes, I would like that," she replied.

They both sat down, opposite each other, sipping coffee waiting to see who would go first. "I wanted to say sorry, for what I did to you all those years ago. It was a time when I had a big ego and an attitude to match. It's no excuse, I know. What I mean to say is, I was totally in the wrong and I am sorry for all the distress that I caused you," he said waiting for her response.

"I would like to thank you for your honesty and courage to admit that you were in the wrong Peter, and you were very much in the wrong. I would like us to draw a line under the past and start afresh," she said.

"I drink to that," he replied raising his coffee.

Over the next few hours, Suzanne and Peter worked tirelessly, eating fast food and plenty of coffee. They put together a task board and team with the current up-to-date information from the crime scene.

Chapter 18

Faith managed to walk about two miles up the road, but kept back-tracking to the farm. She then realised it would be the wrong decision to make, then turned back again and headed back towards town. The boys would enter her mind with a thousand questions and not many answers, and then the emotional guilt and heavy heart would follow, so again she would turn and head back to the farm.

She was about half way back to the farm when she heard a car approaching behind her, beeping a horn. She turned and as the car approached, she realised it was Mitch beeping and flashing his lights. Her heart skipped a beat and she started to run towards the approaching car, wiping the tears away from her cheeks.

Mitch stopped the car and then ran to her, wrapping her up in his arms, squeezing her tightly. "How did you know?" said Faith in floods of tears.

"Matthew, he phoned me on the mobile."

"Matthew, how did he know where I hid the phone?" she said sniffling.

"Apparently, you're not very good at keeping secrets; in fact, you're just rubbish," he said, with a chuckle in his voice, wiping her tears away with his thumbs.

"I have to go back. The boys, I can't leave the boys."

"You can't go back, at least not now. He is angry, upset and getting madder by the minute and if you go marching on back to the farm with all fists blazing, it will all kick off again. Give him and yourself time to calm down."

"But the boys…"

"I'm thinking of the boys. They will be fine, he won't hurt them—he won't hurt them," he said, pulling her closer to him, squeezing even more tightly.

They got in the car and drove off towards the town in silence. Mitch lived on the outskirts of town. His house was painted a beautiful ivory, the gardens landscaped; it also had a pool with BBQ and outside dining area. The house had been in his family for three generations, all doctors as their profession, with each generation putting their own stamp on the place making it their own.

The interior was modern and relaxing. Faith really loved his house; she always felt at home whenever she was here. "You go and run yourself a bath and I will make coffee. I will bring it to you," said Mitch, kissing her forehead, then walked into the kitchen. "Mitch, I haven't any change of clothes?"

"Yeah, you do, they are in the wardrobe on the left hand side," he replied.

"O, I forgot," she said.

Once the bath was filled and full of bubbles, Faith slid into the water. She felt all the weight lift from her shoulders. About five minutes later, Mitch joined her with coffee. "Are you coming in?"

"I can't babe; I have to go to the surgery for a couple of hours, then I will be back. Will you be ok?"

She nodded. "The quicker you go, the faster you will be coming home," she said and with that, he kissed her and left. She rested back in the bath crying, wiping away the tears. She felt tired, she closed her eyes and within seconds she was snoozing.

***

Matthew took on the role as adult in a matter of minutes. He got Mark and Henry dressed and told them to do their chores around the farm with no mucking about. The younger boys did as they were told; putting on their wellies, they headed outside.

Seeing their father at the kitchen table, drinking Jack Daniels from the bottle like it was coca cola, scared them to death and they didn't want to provoke or upset him any further. Matthew started to clean and clear up the house. Anything broken, he put in the bin outside and then he got out the hoover from the cupboard, only for his father to shout at him so he decided to put it away and got the broom out instead.

John staggered out of the house and got into his truck, then drives away. Matthew watched his father drive away. He took out the mobile phone from his pocket and was about to call Mitch Moody but thought better of it, knowing that it would upset his father. So he carried on clearing up the house and farm. Once he had done his chores and checked on his brothers, he decided to plough and seed the top fields. From the age of eight, he learnt how to use the machinery and before long it was second nature to him. It was all he wanted to do, to farm and be like his dad, though the latter part Matthew had started to question.

Lunch came and went, and there was still no sign of his dad or his mum, for that matter. It was 3:45 pm when the mobile phone rang. It was his mum.

"Hi Mummy, where are you?"

"Hi baby, are you boys ok? I am staying with Mitch," she said trying to hold back the tears.

"We are okay, Mummy; Henry and Mark have just finished their chores and now are playing. Mum, when are you coming home?"

"Soon baby, soon. Where's your dad?"

"Oh, he is in the fields, we managed to sow six acres today," he knew it was a lie that he told, but he told it anyhow as he didn't want her to worry. Truth is, he only managed to sow two acres.

"I love you all, and miss you very much," she said tearfully.

Matthew told her he cleaned and cleared up the house and that his brothers are okay and seemed to have gotten over the mornings' events and are as normal. "I have to go now, Mummy there is a car approaching. I love you!"

"I love you too, and I promise you, Matthew, we will all be back together soon," she said then hung up the phone.

***

A woman and young girl got out of the car. They saw a boy starting to approach them in the distance, "Which one am I to have, Mummy?"

"It doesn't matter, just as long as we can keep a roof over our heads, the better. If we keep the father drunk and the eldest son sweet, then I reckon we can call this place home, and it is a lovely house. If we do this right, I think we can cash in here sweetie."

"What about the wife?"

"No need to worry about her, to what I hear Mitch Moody has got his claws into her. The whole town is talking about it. There will be a custody battle for the boys, she will win. All we have to do is secure our position with the father, with you getting pregnant. I will make sure the boys spend as much time with the ex-wife as possible."

"What if he or the son doesn't like me?"

"The son, I am not too sure about, yet. However the father, he would be too drunk to care."

"Here we go," said the woman.

"Hello, I am Matthew. Can I help you?" staring at the young female with all doe eyes.

He couldn't stop staring at her; she was lovely, her dark straight hair was perfect. She wore a white cotton lace dress that come down to her thighs exposing her long thin tanned legs, with red flip-flops finishing off the look. Matthew had never looked at a girl like this before. He felt awkward.

"Yes, I am Tina and this is my daughter, Chloe."

"Chloe," he said, not realising he said her name like a little boy who had a crush on his teacher. Tina looked at him admiring her beautiful daughter which brought a big cheesy smile to her face.

"Hello," replied Chloe.

"We are moving in. Your father kindly asked us to live with you boys. Apparently your mother has gone off with another man and left you boys to fend for yourselves," said Tina.

"What! You are moving in?" said Matthew.

"Yes, it was agreed about an hour ago, be so good and help us with our bags and I will put a pot of tea on the stove and then we can get to know each other."

Matthew did as he was told and took the bags into the house placing them at the foot of the stairs. "Mark and Henry, you won't see them till later, they are out playing."

"Oh, that's fine, so you're the eldest?" said Tina

"Yes, then Henry and then Mark," replied Matthew.

"It was so good of your father to let us stay for a while; I was at my wits' end, wondering where we would go. You see the lease on our apartment had come to an end and the landlord wanted us out. So here we are. I'm sorry this had to happen at such a bad time," said Tina rubbing the top of Matthews's hand.

Tina poured the tea for her, Chloe, and Matthew when John walked in, carrying boxes and more sober than when he left. "Since when did you start having tea Matthew?" said John. Making Matthew blush and feel all embarrassed in front of Tina and Chloe. "Mum, let me have tea sometimes," he replied. John shook his head and murmured under his voice as he started to carry Tina's and Chloe's belongings up the stairs.

"Chloe, I will put you in the guest bedroom and your mum will be in my room. It's the second door on the left. Tina, yours will be the first door on the left. Is that ok?" said John. Both women looked at each other and smirked. "Yes, that's fine, where will you be sleeping," they both replied. "I will be in the guest room just off there."

Tina took a sip of her tea and then followed John upstairs. "What is going to happen to all of Faith's belongings?"

"It will be all be bagged up and gone within the hour."

"Would you like me to do it for you?"

"No, that's fine, I'll do it," he said rubbing his eye.

"I'll leave you to it," and with that Tina headed back down stair to collect some more bags and took them to Chloe's room and started to un-pack them. The room was nice enough, and you could tell that it wasn't used that often. "Could do with a lick of paint and some nice furnishings?" she thought to herself.

Chloe was wrestling with the last of the bags and a box. "Let me help you," said Matthew. He took the box from her and she carried the bag. She kept stopping on the stairs and bending over saying the bag was too heavy, walking up behind her Matthew got an eyeful of her womanhood every time she bent over. He felt ashamed at looking, but excited all at the same time. He had never seen the female genitalia before, and he wanted to touch it. He thought to himself, *My friends are never gonna believe me when I tell them.*

He put the box down on the bed and left at quick speed. Chloe smiled at her mum, "Putty in my hands that one. Good thinking, Mum. I did what you said to do and took the knickers off, worked like a treat. I will be popping his cherry by the end of the week."

Chloe took a good look around her room and started to place her belongings where she wanted them. "Why aren't you unpacking your clothes, Mum?"

"Oh, John is in there packing away all of Faith's stuff, which reminds me, I picked up some of her perfume for you to wear."

"Mum, do I have to wear it? Can't I just seduce him on my own terms?"

"No, he is besotted with her and I have also noticed that the two of you are very similar in looks, a little tweak here and there and you will be Faith's younger self."

"Mum really, can't you go after the father and then I will concentrate on the son."

"No, and we have been over this a thousand times. I mean, looking at him, don't you find him attractive?"

"Yes, he is a sexy guy and with an awesome physique, I just don't think I can pull it off."

"Like I said, a tweak here and there, with the perfume and lace cami nightie I got you, he will be yours in no time at all."

"What about Matthew?"

"The father first, and if that doesn't work, then go after the son."

That night, John put Henry and Mark to bed and left Chloe and Matthew to their own devices whilst he took Tina to work and had a few drinks at the bar at the same time. He didn't want to stay long but Tina made sure he had plenty to drink. Matthew called his mum on the mobile.

Mitch Moody walked into the pub with a couple of friends. He saw John at the bar and decided to stay well clear. Once they got their drinks, they sat in the corner of the pub. Finishing their first round, it was Mitch's turn to go to the bar. Tina served him.

"Hello, doctor."

"Hello Tina, how are you?"

"Fine now, though the day didn't start off as fine. Me and my Chloe got evicted this morning, didn't have no place to go until John kindly took us in."

"You're living up at the farm?"

"Yes, moved in this afternoon. It's only temporary until I can get us sorted. It's a shame I couldn't meet his wife. I understand she is lovely."

"How are the boys?"

"Oh, they are fine. A little bit confused, though I think. Matthew has taken a shine to my Chloe. I hear Faith is staying with you, is that right?"

"Yes, that's right but only as a friend until she can get herself sorted."

A grunted laugh was heard from across the bar. "Ha, friend is that what you call it?" said John.

"That's right, friends."

"Did you know Tina, our good doctor here has been fucking my wife on and off for nearly ten years now."

"No, I didn't know that, I thought it was a recent thing."

By this time, the whole room went quiet and everyone was watching.

"What a fucking mug, I am."

"The only mug around here is Faith for staying with you for as long as she did."

John just grunted and smirked and drank some more Jack Daniels.

"Let's not do this John; I'm sure you don't want the town to know what a bastard you really are."

"I was faithful to her," John shouted, smashing his glass down on the bar.

"You treated and beat her like a dog and let's not mention the abuse you inflicted on Jake," Mitch replied in a loud voice.

John lunged himself at Mitch and punched him in the jaw. Mitch lost his footing and fell backwards. Mitch got to his feet, his hand rubbing his jaw. He saw John standing there with his fists clenched, up near his nose with his heel slightly lifted off the ground, but looking a bit wobbly and unsteady. Mitch walked up to him pushed his fists out of the way and grabbed him by the throat, lifting him and then threw him across the room. John impacted the top of the table which broke in half and he fell to the floor. Mitch walked through tables pushing them out of his way. The occupants of the tables scrambled in all sorts of directions but were still watching all the commotion.

Mitch grabbed him by his shirt. "Those boys better be packed and ready by 08:00 tomorrow or else!"

"You will never get my boys," John said, all gurgled.

"They better be ready," letting John go watching him fall to the ground. Mitch got up and went over to his friends and then they all left.

Tina rushed up to John to see if he was okay. She wiped down his face and helped him up. "Bar's closed, everyone out," she said turning back to John. "Let's get you home and cleaned up."

***

By the time Tina and John arrived back at the farm, other than the porch lights all other lights were off in the house. "I'm going to kill her," John kept saying. "You're drunk."

"They aren't taking my boys."

"You won't have a say in it, the law is on her side."

"They aren't taking my boys!"

"You need to think about what you are saying, c'mon let's get you in the house and have a coffee."

Tina put on the coffee while John sat at the kitchen table with his head in his hands and started to cry like a baby. He didn't notice Tina putting the coffee on the table then disappearing upstairs to bed.

Chloe heard three taps on the door, her mum popped her head around the door. "You're up; you know what you need to do." Chloe made a big sigh and got out of bed. She applied the perfume and slipped on the navy lace cami and headed downstairs.

"Oh my, John, you ok?" she said, placing her hand on his shoulder. He looked up at her and she saw tears streaming down his face. "John, what's happened?"

"I've lost everything," he said, taking a sip of his coffee.

"Oh John, come here," she said, pulling him to her, wrapping her arms around him and let him cry.

John's tears soaked her cami. "I'm sorry," he said, wiping his face and pulling himself away from her. "Do you always dress like that?" John said, getting up from his chair, taking his coffee with him.

"Yes, I didn't expect anyone to be down here. I wanted a glass of water."

"The perfume you're wearing, its Faith's favourite."

"It's my favourite too; Mum brought it for me for my birthday."

John poured a glass of water and handed it to Chloe. Their fingers touched. "Thank you," she said, taking a sip. John grabbed the bottle of Jack in one hand and the other touched her chin and he walked off to his room.

Chloe waited for a few seconds and was about to turn off the lights and head to bed. She turned off the lights and followed John to his room. She didn't knock; she pressed down on the handle and went in. John was already undressed, naked on the bed, drinking down the Jack.

"What do you want, Chloe?"

"I wanted to make sure you were ok."

"Yeah, right. You think I was born yesterday?" John said, taking another swig of the Jack.

"Okay then, I want you; I want you inside me."

"And you think by wearing my wife's perfume and looking like her, we will be having sex."

"No. Not at all; I know I look like her by the photos I have seen around the house," she said, approaching him.

"You look too much like her," he said, staring at her.

Chloe climbed onto the bed kneeling on her knees and was about to remove the lace camisole, "Leave it on." Chloe kissed his lower legs making her way to his thighs, spreading his legs, seeing his cock stiffen; she licked and sucked on his shaft. His eyes rolled and deep down in his throat, he let out a groan of pleasure, taking another swig of the Jack, then placing it on the floor beside the bed.

He pulled Chloe to him, rolling on top of her. "You smell like her," he kissed her on the lips, "you look like her," he kissed her again, "you will never be her!" he said, giving her a deeper, hungrier kiss.

"Fuck me, say her name John, and fuck me." He slipped his hard throbbing cock inside of her calling out Faith's name.

***

It was 6 in the morning when John woke, looking over at Chloe. *Shit,* he thought. He got up knocking over the empty Jack Daniels' bottle and headed to the shower. Once dressed, he got upstairs and checked on the boys. Henry and Mark were fast asleep, but Matthew was up and dressed, sitting at his table, reading his comic.

"Hey sport, why up so early?"

"I couldn't sleep, and was about to go and feed the animals."

"You don't need to do that."

"I know but I like to and you need the help. You can't afford any more help."

"Listen Matt, we need to talk," John said sitting on the edge of the bed. "Come and sit next to me."

"Dad, I know what you are going to ask. I want to stay with you, I don't want to leave the farm. I love Mummy but I don't want to leave the farm."

"How did you know what I was going to ask?"

"Shaun at school went through the same thing when his parents split up. He had to choose."

"Are you sure, because you have to be sure, sport?"

"I am sure, though Mark and Henry will be better off with Mummy."

"No, if you're not going, they aren't either."

"Dad, can't you and Mummy work things out. Why do you have to split up?"

"It's a long story mate and I have fucked up big time. I don't think there is any going back, but I will try and sort things out."

"You need to prepare yourself that she isn't going to come back," John said with tears in his eyes. "You know, if you change your mind, don't be scared to say. I won't get angry all I want is what's best for you guys. Your mum is coming over this morning at eight, with Doctor Moody," said John, as he put his hand onto Matthew's shoulder and gave it a rub and pat. Then, he left the room and went down stairs.

***

A metallic silver Mercedes pulled up in front of the farmhouse; Faith and Mitch get out of the car, the front door opened and all three boys came running out of the house calling, "Mummy, Mummy." Faith's heart sprung back into life as the boys wrapped their arms around her, with lots of kisses, hugs, laughter and tears. Mark and Henry grabbed her by the hand and took her into the house. Hesitantly and full of fear, she entered the house and into the kitchen where John sat at the table. "Hi," she said, with her heart entering her throat.

"Hello," John said, standing there in a daze wanting the world to swallow him up, looking her up and down from head to toe. Feeling, knowing, how much he had missed her even in such a short space of time and he was determined to win her back, not just for him but for their boys.

"Hello, Doctor Moody."

"Hello Matthew, how are you?"

"I am fine, under the circumstances. Are you not coming in?"

"No, this is something your mum has to sort out; I am here as moral support only."

"Or if things get out of hand, you mean…"

"Something like that," turning and placing his arms on top of the hood, staring up at the house.

"I will be staying here with Daddy. He asked me this morning what I wanted to do and I want to stay here."

"What about Mark and Henry?"

"Daddy said if I stay, they stay."

"This is going to break your mum, Matthew."

"And if we go, it will break my dad," said Matthew, heading back into the house.

"Would you like coffee?"

"Yes, please," she said, sitting down at the kitchen table with Mark and Henry, touching their hair and faces like she hadn't seen them for years.

"The house seems different somehow."

"Less furniture, we smashed it up."

"I hear you have taken some lodgers?"

"Yes, but not lodgers, it's only a temporary thing until they find somewhere else."

"Where's Mitch?"

"Waiting in the car," she said, looking around the kitchen.

John put the coffees on the table and sat down. There was an awkward silence.

"You look different."

"You look beautiful," he said, seeing her blush.

"How did we get to this John? How did this happen to us?" she said, sipping her coffee.

"I'm sorry; I failed you and the boys."

"We failed each other."

"Come home, Faith, please come home baby. We can sort this out, I can change!" he said, crying into his hands.

"I'm here for the boys John, I want them with me," she said, tearfully. John wiped his tears away. "They are staying here Faith; uprooting the boys wouldn't be good for them. Ask them yourself, they want to stay here with me at the farm."

"Matthew?" he said.

"I want to stay here, Mum, at the farm with Daddy. Mummy, please come home."

"I can't baby, I can't come home. I can't do that," she said, with tears streaming down her face. Putting his little hand in hers, she squeezed it tightly. Her heart broken and her soul in turmoil, looking at her boys with tearful sore eyes, feeling and seeing her whole world had just collapsed around her.

"Faith, I won't stop you seeing them. You can have them every day after school and every other weekend."

"It's not enough John; I don't want to be a part-time mum."

"Then come home, you belong here with us!"

"John, please don't make things difficult."

"I promise you things will be different."

"Promises I have heard many times before and still it didn't change anything."

"Boys, please go and pack your things; you're coming with me," Faith said wiping her face.

"Stay where you are. They are staying here!" John said with a raised voice.

Faith got up from the table and started to head upstairs. John grabbed her arm. "Faith, don't look at them, you're frightening them!"

"I'm frightening them?" she said angrily, looking over at them her face dropped, seeing them huddled in the corner with

Matthew's arms wrapped around them for protection, their little faces had gone white as a sheet.

"They want to stay here, and there is nothing you can do about it."

"You son of a bitch, damn you, you bastard," shoving his arm away from her. He grabbed her by the hips and pressed her up against the wall, groin against groin, putting his legs in-between hers, he drank her in and felt the softness of her hair. His lips caressing her neck, he felt her becoming aroused.

"Come home baby, we love you!" she cried into his shoulder and he held her tightly. "I'm sorry Faith, I am so sorry for everything, please come home," he whispered into her ear, and then let her go. She staggered out the front door towards the car, not looking back. The ache in the pit of her stomach hurt like nothing she ever felt in her life. She left a broken woman.

Chapter 19

Jake felt on top of the world, he felt untouchable; he had gotten rid of any evidence associating him with the killings. He had burnt the clothes, only ashes remained and he even disposed of them by spreading them around in the cornfield, destroyed the trainers by ripping the sole from the main body then burnt them until nothing was left and again disposing of the remnants in the farmers' fields. Anything that was burnable he burned in the old abandoned warehouse and made sure nothing was traceable back to him. He locked himself in the bathroom and cleaned the instruments twice with bleach, then returned them back to their rightful place in the garage and carried on as if nothing had happened.

As the school was closed for a week, the children received schoolwork to do at home. So he and Ella got their heads down and into the books. The murders were on every news channel and in every newspaper. No one let their children out of their sight without supervision, not even to a neighbour's house or in the front gardens. The parents of the murdered children were parading themselves on television now that the six kids had been identified. Jake didn't care much for this and just smirked when he saw them.

Jake didn't take much notice of the coverage and when asked by his grandparents how he felt about it and if he knew the children, he said he knew of them and told them of the altercation he had with Kevin and that they were the school bullies; they were the ones that attacked Ella.

Ella and Jake were in their den, learning Snow White and the Seven Dwarfs for the school play. Ella was cast as the mirror and Jake was cast as grumpy. "Jake," Mary called out.

"Jake," she called again. "Yes, nana, I'm coming," Jake was not amused at being disturbed and walked out of the den. "Jake you need to come home. There are some people here to see you," she said, holding out her hand.

"What people, nana?"

"Police officers, darling."

Jake's legs went to lead. He wasn't scared but had he prepped enough for this moment, he thought. Would he be believable? He knew it was inevitable before the police turned up on his doorstep. "Hello Jake, I am Inspector Jenson and this is my colleague Inspector Rankin, Would you mind if we asked you some questions?" Jake shrugged his shoulders in indifference and sat down at the dining room table along with his grandparents.

"Jake, we are speaking to all the children at the school and wanted to know if you knew the six children?" said Inspector Jenson.

"I knew of them," Jake said, looking down at his hands.

"Jake, some of the other children said that there was some trouble between you and Kevin Stones on Friday morning at school," said Inspector Jenson.

"Yes."

"What happened?"

"They said they were going to get me after school, and do to me what they did to Ella," said Jake, crying into his hands, whilst being comforted by the grandmother.

"Did you tell a teacher?"

"No."

"Why not?"

"I was scared," he said, still crying.

"Could you tell me what happened next, Jake?"

"They chased me after school, into the woods."

"Did they catch up with you?"

"No, I ran into the woods to the road on the other side and kept running towards the creek. I ran through the creek and then onto Fosdyke Road and then ran home."

"Were the kids still chasing you at this point?"

"I don't think so, I looked back and didn't see anybody; I just carried on running."

"Jake, have you seen anything or anybody acting strange, hanging around the school?"

"No."

"Did you see anyone else in the woods?"

"No."

"Did you tell your grandparents that you were being chased?"

"Yes, I told them it was the same kids that beat up Ella."

"We can confirm that when he got home on Friday, much later than usual, must have been around 4:45 pm, he was distraught and shaking like a leaf and his school clothes were in a state," said Mary, with Mac nodding in agreement.

"Thank you Jake, for your help," said Inspector Jenson.

"Okay Jake, off you go now, back to Ella's," said his grandmother. They all watched Jake leave the house. Mary poured some more tea.

"It's a shame he was running scared. Jake would have been about the last person to see them alive other than the person that killed them all," said Inspector Jenson sipping her tea.

"I just don't understand it, how anyone could do such a dreadful thing," said Mary, trying to hold back the tears, dabbing her eyes with her handkerchief.

Chapter 20

Back at the station Suzanne and Peter slumped at their desks drinking coffee in silence. "Go on, say it, you know you want to," said Suzanne.

"We have nothing, no forensics, no evidence, no leads; all we have is six dead bodies."

"So much having this wrapped up in no time, eh Peter."

"The last possible person that saw them alive was Jake Evans."

"So we have a window of opportunity, don't we?"

"What do you mean?"

"3:15 pm school bell sounds, Jake arrives home around 4:45 pm so that's an hour and half, give or take a little."

"Is there any CCTV on those roads?"

"I doubt it; it's mainly farm land and trees around that area."

"It's worth checking with the highways and the farmers, just in case."

"Keep the team going door-to-door, taking statements from everybody, I want to know if anyone has seen anything unusual, suspicious; this is a small community and if there is anyone that doesn't fit, they will stick out like a sore thumb," said Suzanne.

"We are about to start pulling in the local crims, anyone who has a background in sexual assault, violence and gang related murders."

"What makes you think it was gang related, Peter?"

"I don't. I am assuming, so far, by over half of the statements taken from the local children, they were being bullied and terrorised on a daily basis; basically, we had six kids running around like a pack of wolves, terrorising anyone and anything that crossed their path and the parents didn't have a clue what their kids were up to, when they were out of the house."

"Did any of the children tell their parents or school teachers?"

"No, they were too frightened."

"When will you receive the list?"

"Within the next hour. Sergeant Melody is working on it, as we speak."

"Good."

***

Brandon Radcliffe was different from his peer group; at the age of thirty-one he had an IQ of a fourteen year old. His birth was difficult, with both mother and child nearly at death's door; it was a miracle that both had survived. Being the youngest of three boys, he was a loner, spent most of his time on his own, collecting things that had no interest to anyone else. He kept his hobby tucked away neatly in the shed that his dad had built for him.

He didn't like the city, too noisy and dirty, the traffic and air pollution would not only bring on his asthma but also brought on his migraines that would last for days on end. So he kept himself in the countryside amongst nature and the quiet where he felt comfortable. The only time he had to venture into the city would be for medical appointments.

He had a terrible stutter, and was unable to converse with people, as they would get impatient with him or finished his sentence for him. So he stayed quiet and only answered with either a yes or no response in company. He had the same mullet hairstyle since he was a teenager and wouldn't change it, despite the pleas from his parents. He was polite, well-mannered, with a cheeky air about him.

Brandon's behaviour was quizzical every time the news covered the murders. He became perplexed and confused. When Natasha Cley's name was mentioned, he would giggle and snigger, then become worried and confused. His parents looked at each other, bewildered. "What's gotten you so bewildered, Brandon?"

"N–N–N–tahsa C–C–Cley, sh–sh–sh is m–m my gi–gir fr–fr–rend."

"Don't be silly, you don't have a girlfriend," his father said.

"Y–Y–Yes sh–sh is, w–w–we had s–s–sex, sh–sh–she held my ha–ha–hand and we kissed," he said.

"You what? When was this Brandon?" his mother asked.

"O–on F–F–ri–Friday lu–lunch."

"Last Friday lunch?" said his father.

"Yes."

His mum and dad looked at each other.

"How long has this been going on?" his mum said.

"M–m–months."

"And where do you both have sex?" said his father

"I–ii–in the w–w–woods, w–w–we have a–a–a tent w–where w–w–we all g–g–go."

"What do you mean by we? Who else were there with you Brandon?"

"K–K–Kev."

"Kevin Stones?" said his mother in amazement. Brandon nodded.

"Shit, this is bad. I need to think. Did you use a condom?" Brandon shook his head.

"Shit, shit, you stupid fucking idiot," his father said, getting up from his chair pacing the room whilst rubbing the back of his neck with Brandon watching him becoming more and more frightened.

"It's only a matter of time before they come knocking, we need to get you out of here!" his father said.

"Now, don't be too hasty," his mother said.

"What do you mean?"

"Well, if they find his DNA on her, and if he disappears, then he becomes a wanted man with his face in every newspaper and on every television news channel in the world and they will throw the book at him," his mother said in frustration. "Our only hope for Brandon is to go to the police and tell them everything and pray."

"You mean get in there first; we are going to need a fucking good lawyer," his father said, sitting back down in his chair with his hands pressed together resting against his chin. "How could you be so stupid?" His father said shaking his head.

Brandon sat in silence listening to his parent's conversation but not understanding the magnitude of the situation and his involvement. Even in his confused state he could see that they meant trouble was coming which sent a cold chill throughout his body.

***

"G'day, may I help you?" said the office behind the counter. His grey complexion and sloping facial features on the left side of his face indicated that the officer had had a stroke. His overweight body restricted his movements.

"Yes we have information with regards to the murdered kids and we would like to talk to someone, please," he said.

"May I take your name, sir?"

"Yes, Trevor Radcliffe and this is my wife, Pam, and our son, Brandon."

"If you would take a seat, someone will be with you shortly," the officer said. Watching them take a seat, he picked up the telephone and made a call to Inspector Jenson.

Ten minutes passed then Inspector Jenson entered the front desk and escorted Mr and Mrs Radcliffe and Brandon into interview room one. Within two minutes, Inspector Rankin entered the room.

"You told the front desk you had information for us regarding the murders?" Inspector Jenson said.

"Yes, our son Brandon was with Natasha Cley and Kevin Stones on the day of the murders. It seems they were in a sexual relationship." Inspector Jenson read Brandon his rights and postponed the interview until his solicitor arrived.

After intensive interrogation, Inspector Jenson and Rankin postponed the interview. Making her way back from the chief super's office with a signed warrant to search the premises of the Radcliffe household, she entered the Interview Room One and requested Mr and Mrs Radcliffe to accompany them to their home, leaving Brandon with his solicitor.

They arrived at the Radcliffe home around 11:45 am. "Mr and Mrs Radcliffe, I am holding a warrant to search these premises and any other premises you hold. Could you tell us where Brandon's room is, please?"

Completely in shock surrounding the turning of events Mrs Radcliffe could barely speak, sitting down on her couch with her head in her hands, in tears, with her husband's arm around her, trying to console her, watching the police officers going through their personal things that they held dear. Feeling violated and sickness developing in the pit of his stomach, "It's the first left through that door; he also has his own space with the shed at the bottom of the garden."

"Thank you, Mr Radcliffe."

"What's happening, I don't understand. We came to you."

"Ma'am, you better come and see this," the constable said as he walked through the back door.

Entering the shed at the bottom of the garden, Inspectors Jenson and Rankin couldn't believe what they were seeing. "We need forensics, I will call them," said Inspector Rankin. "Ma'am, Ma'am," Inspector Jenson heard her name being called repeatedly. She cleared the shed of persons, shut and bolted the door, so the contents would not be contaminated.

Inspector Jenson entered Brandon's room. There was clothing everywhere, the bed was unmade and the television was still on. However, the picture was on pause and the smiling face looking back at her was of a naked Natasha Cley's. "Looks like we have got our man!" she said, under her breath. She cleared the room in readiness for forensics.

Heading back into the living area, "Mr and Mrs Radcliffe, could you accompany me back down to the station please?"

"Eh, yes, why?!" Mr Radcliffe said with Mrs Radcliffe looking bewildered as though she has just entered her worse nightmare.

"Mr and Mrs Radcliffe, I am arresting you on suspicion of murder, you do not have to say anything. But, it may harm your defence if you do not mention when questioned something which you later rely on in court. Anything you do or say may be given in evidence."

The couple were separated and taken to the police station in separate cars. Forensics arrived. Police cordoned off the area. Within a couple of hours, items were tagged and bagged and were placed in the back of a white transit van.

***

Mr and Mrs Radcliffe were released after four hours of being interviewed by the police. They were told they weren't allowed to go back to their home, but had to find alternative accommodation within the area for a while until the police were finished gathering evidence.

They stayed with close friends, looking grey and dishevelled from their former selves, walking around like ghosts, only talking amongst themselves and very close family and friends. Mrs Radcliffe lost a stone overnight and Mr Radcliffe, with intense grief, brought on a heart attack, which would affect him for the rest of his life.

Their other two sons arrived from Sydney and Melbourne to support their younger brother and parents. They had to find themselves a new home and start again. Once it got out and the police had finished gathering their evidence, their home was set on fire and burned to the ground. People looked at them strangely, whispering behind their backs whilst others swore obscenities at them and spat on the ground. People they had known all their lives avoided them and wouldn't speak to them. When the police were satisfied they had nothing to answer for, they were released without further charges and were then allowed to go about their business.

Kevin Stones' home was also raided. As they entered the house, they found Mrs Stones destroying the evidence in the shed and was arrested and charged with facilitating in child sex exploitation and abuse. The police confiscated hundreds of DVDs and a video camera that was found in the garden shed. They also found one hundred thousand dollars in cash, stashed in the filing cabinet along with contact numbers, names, addresses and dates. Young Molly was placed in a foster home with a family that could attend to her needs.

The tent in the woods was tagged and bagged as evidence. They found used condoms and discarded knickers which belonged to Natasha Cley.

Brandon Radcliffe was charged with the murders of, Kevin Stones, Justin McClure, George Bradshaw, Heather Cilliërs, Wilf Macintosh and Natasha Cley. His name would be placed on the child sex register and he was sentenced to life imprisonment without parole.

The evidence provided in court was so devastating, Mr and Mrs Radcliffe couldn't sit through it. Watching their son with his head down, looking sullen and terrified, they felt sick, disgusted and ashamed of their son, with the mounting evidence piling up against him. Unable to rationalise that their son was a deviant, an animal, they didn't know this man standing in front of them.

Police trawled through hundreds of hours of DVDs to discover young Molly Stones subjected to devilish disgusting sexual treatment by adult men and women. She had been exploited for years; some of the men and women had now been identified and were in the process of being prosecuted. Natasha Cley and Heather Cilliërs were also found on the tapes, exploited by the same men and women.

In the tapes found at the home of Brandon Radcliffe, the content was of him and Natasha Cley. The bloodstained clothing found in the shed and personal items belonging to Natasha Cley were identified by the family. Semen was also found in the body. The most significant was the silver diamond bracelet that belonged to her late maternal grandmother.

The court heard of how this gang of kids terrorised and frightened the old and young. Walking around the streets like a pack of wolves hunting for their prey. Anyone they came in contact with, who they believed was an easy target, was subjected to verbal abuse and violence.

Brandon cried and pleaded with the Judge as his sentence was passed. He was then taken away.

Inspector Suzanne Jenkins was praised and promoted to Super Chief Inspector. She made it her mission to expose, chase and arrest the men and women identified on the DVDs, exposing a paedophile and sex trafficking ring. Wanting justice!

Chapter 21

Matthew scoured at his father, "She is too young for you, you love Mum. Why haven't you tried to sort things out?"

"Because your mother doesn't want to be with me," he said, turning the page of the local newspaper, "and besides she has been cheating on me for years with the local quack. What makes you think I want her back?"

"Because you are in love with her."

"Love isn't everything, Matthew. I treated her badly, son, shamefully bad. Sometimes you can't be forgiven for that."

"I take it you have a thing for young Chloe then?"

"No!"

John laughed at Matthew, shaking his head in amusement. Getting up from the kitchen table, he started to head to the back door and turned, "Listen Matt, you like Chloe and that's fine, but don't lose your head, like her mother, that one."

"What do you mean?"

John didn't answer but just left the house leaving Matthew standing in the kitchen. John saw a car approaching in the distance; he knew it would be Faith, no doubt coming to collect the rest of her stuff. Even so, his heart fluttered and he felt all giddy.

Faith parked the car and John opened the door. "Hello," she said, looking at him, all quizzical. "Looks like you have found your vocation, you look really good in this car," drinking in her scent as she walked past him. Wanting to wrap her up in his arms and never wanting to let her go, she said, "Where are the boys?"

"The youngest two are with friends, out for the day and Matt's in the house," as he said that Matthew came running from the house wrapping his arms around his mother, squeezing her tightly, "I love you, Mum."

"And I love you," kissing him on the forehead.

"Coffee?" said John.

"Yes, please."

"Matt, please go and put the kettle on."

Matthew did as he was told, leaving his mum and dad alone. "So where's the boyfriend?"

"So where's the girlfriend," she snapped back at him. John could only say, "Matthew?" She nodded rolling her eyes. "I have no defence, I was drunk, and she was wearing your perfume and some sexy underwear. What's a man to do, I'm not made of wood."

"Still a bit of self-control wouldn't go amiss. Seventeen, John. She is fucking seventeen," raising her hands in frustration.

"Jealous," shrugging his shoulders.

Faith walked off in the direction of the house, shaking her head and swearing under her breath.

Entering the house, Matthew was making coffee, "And when did you start drinking coffee, Matthew?" thinking to herself, *I haven't been gone long and things have changed so much.*

"I wanted one, is that ok?"

"Sure, but only half a cup."

Matthew poured the coffees and sat down at the table with his parents. Matthew started to drink and in quick succession spat the coffee back out into the cup. Both his parents looked at each other and laughed. Matthew got monk on; he went to the fridge to get some bottled water and stormed out of the house, listening to his parents laughing at him. Faith, not thinking, put her hands in his, bringing his hand up to her mouth and kissed the back of his hand.

John pulled her onto his lap and they kissed. The gentle touch of his soft lips against her skin, his fingers in her hair, the slight touch of skin to skin; she could feel him swelling. She pulled back and just stared into his eyes, which were now filled with tears. "I'll do anything, please come back to me," pressing his face into her chest wrapping his arms around her.

"I have to go," she whispered, pushing him away. Getting off his lap, he held onto one of her hands. "Faith, baby, I know I have done terrible things to you and to Jake. You have to let me try to make amends, to put things right."

"Loving you was never a problem for me, John. When you drink you become someone I don't even know, you're ugly when you drink. I don't like that person, and I can't be around that person."

"I'll change."

"You have been saying that for years, and nothing changes."

John got up off the chair, still holding her hand; he wrapped her back in his embrace and held her tightly, then released her and watched her as she left.

Later that evening, the house was still and quiet. John sat in his bed naked with a bottle of Jack between his legs watching Reservoir Dogs. Chloe entered the room wearing a see-though camisole. "I thought I would come and say hi. You look like you could use the company," she said. "You were absent at dinner, we were wondering where you got to."

John looked at her and laughed, "Wasn't hungry."

"I'm hungry," she said, crawling up the bed on all fours. John picked up the bottle of Jack and took a swig. Chloe pulled back the sheet revealing his swelling penis. She slipped his cock into her mouth, her tongue licking his shaft from tip to base. He grabbed her hair and pulled her up to him. He tore the camisole from her body and slipped himself inside of her, sucking and biting her nipples really hard, bruising them. She rode his cock, hard and fast.

John lifted her, placing her underneath him. "I'm going to show you how I really like it," pumping steadily and deep inside of her, hearing her groans. "Say her name, John, and fuck me!" John looked at Chloe and pulled himself back onto his heels. He slapped her hard around the face bruising her cheek. Before she realised what had just happened, John had his hand around her throat.

He could feel her terror, which excited him. She tried to move but was unable to, she was still straddled to him. She tried to scratch him but was unable to as he grabbed both wrists and pulled them over her head. She was unable to scream due to his hand still around her throat restricting her voice and breath. He could feel her body go limp, giving up the struggle. He let go of her throat and held her wrists, releasing his other hand, reaching down for his belt, he tied her wrists to the bed. "Please, don't hurt me, John," Chloe said whimpering.

John positioned himself more comfortably, "I'm not going to hurt you, I'm going to fuck you, isn't that what you wanted?" he said taking the Vaseline out of the bedside drawer. "No, not like that," trying to move. "The more you resist, the more it will hurt; now just relax," massaging the Vaseline into her ringer then inside of her anus with one finger at first, then inserting two fingers. Before applying more Vaseline he could feel her tense up, he placed his thumb onto her clit, slowly applying pressure in a circular motion whilst still working the anus muscle. "That's it now, I have you." Licking her lips, her body relaxed and moved in unison with his penetrating hand. Applying more Vaseline, a third finger inserted inside of her, stretching her muscle, further penetrating her deeper and deeper, making sure every part of her anus was fully greased and accessible.

Slipping his fingers into her moist pussy alternating both entrances, using her juices to liquefy the Vaseline he then greased his hard throbbing cock and slowly slipped it inside of her anus. Her muscles tightened and locked around his cock; a deep groan released from deep within him as he slowly pulsed inside of her. His breath became slower and deeper as he penetrated her harder and faster.

He could feel his climax building when he pulled his cock from her anus and thrusted himself into her juicy wet pussy. Her pleasure mounted as he pumped deep and hard inside of her; he sucked and bit her nipples hard. Withdrawing again, leaning back on his heels for a breather, he placed his hands onto her hips feeling her skin, whilst his thumbs made their way through her pubic hair, making their way down, opening her outer lips, revealing her clit.

His thumbs were on either side of her clit, applying pressure, squeezing them together, then rubbing her tip with thumb, like a miniature punch bag; her body was shocked with pleasure, her head went side to side with her pleading for more, calling his name. He inserted the vibrator inside of her, positioning the rabbit head onto her clit and turned it on, her body jolted. He lifted her hips to him, her legs over his shoulders. Slipping his cock into her anus he pumped, slowly at first, then faster and harder, her body shuddered into a climax, gushing all over him.

He kept on pumping inside of her, the harder and ferocious he got, the more excited and turned on it made him. Chloe, reaching her second orgasm, was still pleading for more; the harder he pumped, the more she wanted. Spilling his seed inside of her, from head to toe his whole body shuddered. Picking up his t-shirt wiping his cock then throwing it in the wash basket, sitting next to Chloe removing her bonds, she sat up. "You hurt me!" she said, slapping him on the chest.

"It didn't sound like I was hurting you," he said, pushing her away.

"You're a fucking pig," getting up walking to the door.

"Yeah, that's right, and you keep coming back for more," he said, watching the ending of Reservoir Dogs, not acknowledging her.

Chapter 22

Faith was making lunch for her and Mitch, when the doorbell rang. Mitch got up from the dining room table and made his way to the front door. "Hello Doctor Moody, could I see Faith please?"

"Course you can. Come on in, she is in the kitchen."

Walking through to the kitchen, Faith looked up and saw a young girl of seventeen, standing there looking at her. "Hello, I'm…" Before she could say any more Faith interrupted, "Yes, you're Chloe. Have you had lunch?"

"No," Chloe responded, shaking her head.

"Well, then take a seat and I shall get another plate, would you like lemonade, its homemade?"

"Yes, please."

Faith watched the young girl apprehensively move towards the kitchen table awkwardly as if she was in pain or suffered from arthritis in the joints. Faith started to serve and Mitch got the drinks and placed them onto the table.

Chloe drank and ate like she had never been fed; Faith and Mitch just looked at each other in surprise. "What brings you here, Chloe?" Mitch said.

"I wanted to talk to Faith. I need some advice and I can't go to momma. She wouldn't understand and people say you are so kind, so I thought I would take a chance in hope that you would talk to me."

"What seems to be the problem Chloe, what can I help you with?"

"Your husband."

Faith's eyebrow rose as she and Mitch exchanged thoughts and looked telepathically.

"This is my cue to leave," Mitch said, gathering up his drink and plate.

"You don't need to leave on my account, Doctor Moody."

"I think I do. I'll be in the office if you need me," Mitch said, walking out into the hall heading towards his office. Faith turned her attention back to Chloe.

"Chloe, how can I help you?"

"I'm pregnant. I am going to have John's baby."

"Really and how far gone are you?"

"A few weeks."

"Well, it explains your appetite."

"I've come here to tell you to stay away from John and the farm. I don't want to see you up there. It only confuses matters, and it confuses him."

Faith laughed, "You silly, silly little girl. Who put you up to this?"

"No one, I have come here on my own."

"That's not what I asked Chloe. Did your mum put you up to this?"

"No."

"Right, okay, for starters you will see me at the farm as my boys are there and I will only be there to see them."

"Second, you are not carrying John's baby."

"I am carrying his baby; you are just saying that because you are jealous. Jealous of what we have together. You don't want him so now I want you to leave him alone."

"Chloe, honey, you're deluding yourself if you think you will have a future with John. Listen to me, you can't be having his baby because John has had a vasectomy, he can't have any more children."

"You're lying, you're just saying that."

"Chloe, I'm not. He doesn't love you and doesn't want to be with you. He is just using you."

"We are to be engaged, once your divorce comes through."

"Chloe, why did you really come here to see me."

"I wanted to see who Faith Evans really is and I wanted to look you in the eye and tell you to stay away from my family."

"You mean my family Chloe; it is not yours and never will be."

"Stay away Faith or else…" and with that she picked up her fork and stabbed Faith in the back of the hand. Faith screamed and Mitch came running into the kitchen.

"You have been warned, stay away!" Chloe got up from the table and started to walk out of the house. "You know you really aren't that great, average I would say," Chloe left the house and walked up the drive. She got into the passenger side of a black saloon car. Mitch ran from the house after Chloe but was too late; the car drove away. Mitch headed back into the house and tended to Faith's injury, "Crazy fucking bitch, that one," he said.

"Mitch, I'm worried. I'm worried for my boys, and she said she is pregnant."

"If not John, then who is the father?" he said.

"Oh no, Matthew! I bet the little slag is doing them both."

"Surely not."

"I need to go to the farm; I need to speak to John."

"I'll go with you, but tomorrow, not today. We need to go to the hospital and get your hand checked out."

***

Sucking on her nipples, squeezing her buttocks between his fingers as she rode him, with her fingers in his hair, she pulled back his head. "Stick out your tongue," he did as he was told. She brought her mouth to his and sucked on his tongue, sliding him deeper inside of her. He smacked her on the bottom, "On your knees." Entering her hard and fast, pumping so hard, she cried out for him to stop but he didn't, holding her hips, controlling her rhythm, he thrust deeper inside of her until he spilled his seed.

After wiping his cock, he rested back against the headboard then switched the television on. Bored with the company, he took a big drink of Jack. "Don't you think you have had enough of that," he looked at her and took another drink, then went back to watching television. "You need to clean your act up, especially now, now that I am going to be having your baby."

John looked at her, "Not my baby."

"Yes, it's your baby."

"No, it isn't. Now get the fuck out."

"That's what she said before I stabbed her."

"What? Stabbed who?"

"Your ex-wife."

John grabbed her by the throat and made her tell him what happened. He threw her off the bed and onto the floor. Pure rage building up inside of him; he got off the bed and put on his shorts. "I thought it would make you happy, her out of our lives."

"You're fucking delusional," he said, grabbing her chin. "You are a fuck and a lousy one at that, you fucking little slag," punching her in the stomach. With her body reeling in pain, she cradled her womb, "John, please, the baby."

"Who is the father?" getting on top of her with his hands around her throat. "I won't ask again, who is the fucking father?"

"Matthew, Matthew is the father," he let go of her and got off of her.

"Start talking bitch or else…"

"It was Mum's idea."

"Keep going," holding her throat with one of his hands, his eyes full of rage, terrifying her to the bone.

"We gave up the flat, we weren't evicted. The idea was to get pregnant by you or Matthew, that way it would secure us the farm. She said to keep you drinking and keep you sweet so you wouldn't notice us taking it from you. I was to keep you occupied. She said you would be putty in my hands as I resembled your wife. All I had to do was to imitate her, wear her clothes, her perfume. Look after the boys."

"You cunt, you fucking cunt!"

"Who's the cunt John, you're a fucking joke," she said in a maniacal nervous laugh.

Dragging her to the bed, kicking and screaming, Tina came barging into the room, seeing John beating her. "STOP, JOHN STOP," she screamed running towards them, barging John out of the way. "She's pregnant," she said protectively covering her daughter.

"Yeah and don't I just know it. Oh and by the way whose idea was it to visit Faith."

"I don't know, what you mean."

"Yes, you fucking do. Get your stuff and get the fuck out of my house."

"What, did you think it was my baby? Well, you're wrong Tina. I shoot blanks, but you didn't know that, did you?"

"John, she needs a hospital."

"Oh, fuck off, just get out and don't come back."

Tina scoped up Chloe who could barely walk, with a bruised and bloody face and in severe pain, she cradled her lower tummy. She felt disorientated, spaced out and giddy, sobbing into her mother's shoulder. Unable to speak clearly her voice raspy and sore, Tina got her in the car and took her to hospital.

**

John woke from a drunken stupor; he took a shower and headed into the kitchen. Matthew sat at the kitchen table. "I heard everything. I've just called Mum, she is coming to collect us. Henry and Mark are packing."

"I'm sorry Matt, I just seem to keep making mistake after mistake. I am not going to stop you going but I wish you guys would stay."

"We are frightened of you, Dad. You scare us. Since Mum left you have gotten worse."

"I would never hurt you guys, you know that, Son."

"That's just it; we don't, not anymore."

"I'll change Matt, I promise you I will get help, I promise."

"Many times I heard you say that to Mum and nothing changes."

They heard a car approach the house. Faith got out of the car and goes into the house. Mark and Henry took their belongings to the car, they rushed back and gave their dad a massive tearful hug and kisses. Not doing a very good job of holding back the tears, John wrapped them up in his arms and kissed them. "Be good for your mum. I love you both so much," both boys tearfully nodded and left the house still crying in the car.

John grabbed and cocooned Matthew, wrapping his arms around him in a bear hug. "I promise you, I'll change," he whispered. Not wanting to let him go, they both sobbed in each other's arms. "John, John, let him go," Faith said gently placing her hand on John's arm. Reluctant to let go, Faith substituted herself for Matt and took his place. "Go to the car Matt; leave me with your dad."

Holding John tightly in her arms, "Where has the man I loved, gone?" she whispered, kissing his cheek whilst stroking her fingers through his hair. "I promise, I'll change."

"I hope for your sake you do, John," she kissed him on the lips. "Bye, see you soon," she left the house. With the boys securely in the car, she drove away.

Watching them leave with his hands behind his head, his piercing blue eyes were full of tears, heartache and desperation.

It was late afternoon when Tina entered the house and found John slumped in his chair in the living room. "Well, it will please you that Chloe has had a miscarriage."

"Don't you dare make it sound as though it is my entire fault? You shouldn't prostitute your daughter."

"What's that supposed to mean?"

"Oh come on Tina, your little scheme to get your hands on my farm has been rumbled. You're lucky the little slag is still alive. Playing my boy off against me, did you really think you would get away with it?"

"I think you are a very sad drunk, who has nothing left and all he knows is how to bully and beat up women."

"I do hope you have come to get your stuff, anything you leave behind I will burn, now fuck off."

"I feel sorry for anyone who comes in contact with you!" she said, storming upstairs to pack her belongings.

"Touché, bitch," he said under his breath.

***

John spent the rest of the week house bound and drunk. George, his Farm Manager, checked on him once a day just to see if he was still alive and provided Faith with a daily report on his welfare. Otherwise he was left alone to wallow in his own self-pity.

Thursday came and went and still no improvement, Faith's concerns were growing. Getting the boys off to school and Mitch at the surgery, before driving up to the farm she decided to stop at the food hall to get some groceries, she was dreading what she might find. Seeing George in the distance driving the tractor, she waved. Entering the house was a shock to her system, pretty much every room she went in was smashed up, with no sign of John downstairs. She ventured up to the first floor.

The state of the rooms was pretty much as they were downstairs. Only the beds and mattresses were left intact but nothing else; it was all broken, destroyed and there was clothing everywhere. Faith placed her head in her hands and cried. She found John in the bathroom, slumped in the bath on his back, snoring, covered in his own vomit, saliva and shit. The smell of him turned her stomach into retching, trying not to vomit; she opened the window to alleviate some of the smell. She felt angry, frustrated and betrayed; she turned on the shower and soaked him with cold water until he stirred.

Rubbing his eyes and yawning, he saw Faith towering over him. Her face was full of rage; he had never seen her look at him like that before. "You fucking stink, look at the state of you, look what you have done to the house, our memories, our boys' stuff, you selfish fucking bastard," she screamed at him. "Clean yourself up, you're a fucking disgrace," wanting to punch him real hard but instead she threw the shower head at him and went down to the kitchen where she cleaned out the fridge of spoiled food then replenished it with the groceries she had brought with her. She tidied and cleaned a space on the worktop and started to make John something to eat, and put a fresh pot of coffee on.

John stretched and looked down at the state of himself; retching over the smell and the mess as he took off his jeans and t-shirt he cleaned himself up and washed the shit down the plug hole, brushed his teeth and took another shower. He put on his red shorts and t-shirt. He put his soiled clothing in a bag and threw it out of the window, so it could be burned later.

Heading down the stairs and into the kitchen, the smell of food and fresh coffee sent hunger pains into overdrive. He realised he hadn't eaten for days. "Sit down," Faith said, after managing to put together the table using two chairs as supports. "I'm sorry."

"You have been saying that a lot lately," passing him his food which he devoured in seconds. Sitting down next to him, she gave him his coffee. "Feel better?" she said.

"Much, thanks," they both sat in silence wondering who will speak first. "How are the boys?"

"Good, they are good. Missing you, always asking for you."

"I miss them too," he picked up her damaged hand and placed it in his, cradling and kissing it, rubbing his cheek against it with his eyes closed.

"Does the boyfriend know you're here?" he said opening his eyes, staring into hers.

"You really know how to ruin a moment. No, he doesn't and he isn't my boyfriend either."

"You're together, aren't you?"

"No, John we are not together. We are sleeping in separate rooms as a matter of fact."

"But I thought…"

"Well, you thought wrong, didn't you?"

"Are you coming home?"

"Well, you haven't given us anything to come home to, have you. It's gone, and you have destroyed everything, all our memories our precious things."

"Does this mean, you will?"

"You need to get help John. You need to address your issues, and only then we can start talking about our future. But you need to want to do it, only you can change your habits."

"I love you."

"And I love you, I have always loved you," he pulled her onto him wrapping each other in their arms. His heart fluttered and he felt a dark cloud lifting and for the first time in a long time he could see clearly.

***

Later that evening John made himself some food, the house silent and still. Looking across the kitchen, he saw half a bottle of Jack calling him. Wanting, needing him to pick up and have a drink. He walked over to the bottle and picked it up and walked back to the cooker. He was about to take a drink, out of habit but stopped himself and then went over to the sink and poured the contents down the sink. He opened the cupboard where he kept his booze and poured thirty bottles of Jack Daniels and ten bottles of Whiskey down the sink and threw the empty bottles into a black bin bag.

He started with the kitchen and hall, anything that couldn't be salvaged, he threw in the bin. He made a bonfire out the front and stacked broken furniture that couldn't be repaired. Other than the makeshift table in the kitchen, pretty much everything went onto the bonfire. He washed down the walls, surfaces and floors. He did the same with the living room. Making his way upstairs, he picked up all the clothes and anything that wasn't torn went into the wash. He cleaned the house from bottom to top. It was 3 am when he finished.

John went out the front and lit the bonfire and watched it burn. He looked at his watch and realised the time, knowing his guys would be starting work shortly. George arrived twenty minutes later with concern all over his face, "Have you lost your mind?"

"It's never been clearer, George."

"What's happened?"

"Nothing. I'm sober and I have cleared and cleaned the house, she was so upset when she saw it. I'm getting my shit together."

"Come here, you," George who was built like a giant with hands like shovels, squeezed him tightly, his black wavy short hair moving with the breeze. "It's good to have you back."

One by one, the guys turned up to work and all stood around the fire listening to the crackling. "Right okay, get to work you lot," George said, leaving John standing looking into the fire.

John went into the house and made coffee; he waited for the laundry to finish and pegged it out. He took a shower and fell asleep on Matthews' bed.

John woke around mid-day, washed and got dressed. He got out his mobile and looked up Alcoholics Anonymous and spoke to a woman called Laurie. There was a group session on that evening at 7 pm. John wrote down the address and placed it in his pocket.

Chapter 23

"Hi Mum, hi Dad," Faith said, getting out of the car with Mitch and the boys.

"We weren't expecting you till later on," said Mary. Faith wrapped her arms around her parents and squeezed them tightly, "I have missed you both so much. Where's my boy?"

"He is out with Ella and her parents for the day, learning to Ski. We haven't told him, thought we would leave it as a surprise," Mac said, walking over to the boys giving a group bear hug, and then shaking Mitch's hand.

"Dad, you remember Mitch, don't you?" Faith said.

"Yes, I remember. Let's get in and have some refreshments and catch up."

As they all entered the house, Mac and Mary looked at each other as they followed in behind everyone else. They sat around the dining room table and discussed the events over the last few months. "Mum, may I see Jake's room please?"

"Course you can, it's down the hall, last door on the left."

Faith came to the last door with her hand on the doorknob, apprehensive to enter. She took a deep breath and opened the door. She saw a clean tidy room with pictures he had drawn on the walls; *exceptionally talented*, she thought to herself. She opened his wardrobe doors and looked at, and smelled his clothes.

Sitting down on the bed she had tears in her eyes; Mary entered the room and sat next to her putting her arm around her daughter's shoulders. "Oh, I have missed him so much Mum," placing her head onto her mum's shoulder.

"He has grown so much, in many ways, we are so very proud of him."

"I can't wait to hold him."

"How are things really, darling?"

"Oh Mum, everything is so messed up back home, with John drinking himself to death, Matthew almost becoming a father himself."

"W… what did you say?"

"Matthew was almost a father, but the girl had a miscarriage. It's a long story. I will tell you and Dad later when the boys are all in bed. Are you sure you can accommodate all of us?"

"Yes, of course, we will manage. It's not often I get to see my girl," Mary said, stroking Faith's hair.

"Tell me, what is happening with Mitch. Are you two an item now?"

"No, we are going to stay friends. We do love each other deeply, and we have fun. We have talked so much over the last few weeks. Oh Mum, I am so in love with John, never been anyone for me, but him," Mary held Faith more tightly, comforting, cradling her in her arms. "John is an ill man, Faith; hopefully he will find his way back to you."

"I want Jake to come home, Mum."

"That's not a good idea sweetheart. Especially when you are thinking of going back to John; Jake has come a long way in a year."

"But I miss him, Mum."

"I'm sure you do darling, but he isn't going back with you."

Jake arrived home around 6 pm, "Mummy, Mummy," and ran to her, wrapping their arms around each other. "Oh, my darling boy," feeling his face, touching his hair and kissing him all over. "How I have missed you," she said, hugging him tightly.

Matthew, Mark and Henry circled them both into a group hug. "Good to see ya, creep," all three boys said, messing up his hair. Jake took a step back observing who else was in the room.

"Jake honey, you remember Mitch Moody, don't you?" Jake nodded his head, and then said hello to Mitch

135

apprehensively. "Nana, have we got time to play football before dinner?" said Jake. "Yes, I will call when dinner is done," with that the four boys headed out into the garden with Faith watching them through the window.

"Oh, sit down Faith, for Christ's sake," Mary said.

"I just want to watch them, that's all."

"Why don't you concentrate on those potatoes? They won't peel themselves."

"I can do that," said Mitch.

"No, you're on depodding the peas and Mac you're on the carrots."

They all sat round the kitchen table, where Faith told her parents the events that had happened over the last few weeks, now that the boys were playing outside. Mac and Mary shocked and stunned and Mitch and Faith were even more shocked over the children's murders. "The point is everyone has known Brandon Radcliffe since he was born, and never would have thought he was capable of doing such a terrible thing. The community is still in shock and I don't think it will recover. The family have now moved away. I am surprised you haven't seen it on the news," said Mac.

"Well, to be honest, we have been so consumed in our own affairs we have hardly had any time at all to see what else is going on in the country," said Mitch.

"Which makes me even more convinced that Jake should come home now?" Both Mac and Mary exchanged looks. "I have already told you darling, no he isn't."

"Dad…"

"The answer is no, Faith."

"But…"

"When did you become so selfish and self-absorbed?" said Mac.

"What?"

"You heard me. At what point in your brain are you going to think about Jake and put him first?"

"I just thought…"

"That's right, you didn't think; you never think. I blame me and your mother; being an only child, we spoilt you."

"Oh, here we go."

"Don't you dare take that tone with me! Remember what we agreed, would you like me to repeat what we agreed?"

"Things have changed, Dad."

"You will not uproot Jake again. He is settled, leave him be, if you want to do what is right by him, leave him where he is."

"I'm still going to ask him. You can't stop me from asking. I am his mum after all."

"You are testing my patience, that's what you are doing."

"Maybe, it will be best to leave it for a while," said Mitch

"Yes, I agree," said Mary.

Both were feeling very uncomfortable. "Right, let me go and check on the meat," said Mary, getting up from the table. "I'm coming with you," said Mitch, picking up the bowl of peas and carrots whilst Mary took the potatoes and finished them off in the kitchen, leaving Mac and Faith scouring and arguing with each other. "I'm sorry this is my fault," said Mitch.

"Why, what makes you say that?"

"I put the thought of Jake coming home with us."

"Mitch, I have always liked you, ever since you were a boy, which is the reason why I am going to be blunt with you now. Where do you see this relationship going with Faith?"

"I see us together, all of us as a family including Jake. It's been a long time coming."

Mary took a deep breath. "Mitch, I love my daughter, very much, however, she is a drama queen and likes drama in her life, she always has, and no matter what shape it comes in. You, on the other hand, are a sensible guy, her father is a sensible guy also."

"I understand what you are saying."

"No, I don't think you do."

"You think I have rose tinted spectacles on, because I have always loved her."

"What's your earliest memory of Faith regarding the types of men she is attracted to, and those she used to date before she met John?"

"She said she used to date bad boys, violent men, then she met John and he changed everything."

"And John isn't a bad boy?"

"No, he is just a thug who beats women. You saying, Faith likes that?"

"I think John goes too far, however, he knows Faith, he knows who she is, what stimulates her, what she wants and needs, alien to the average normal person, I would even go as far to say, that normal people wouldn't understand it."

"You are telling me to leave her?"

"I'm telling you to be careful or you are in danger of completely losing yourself in a situation you can't get out of, or control."

"I am so in love with her Mary, I always have been. She is great, a brilliant mum, she is beautiful and I am nuts about her."

"Do you think she is in love with you?"

"Yes, she is!"

"I have no doubt that she is fond of you Mitch, but you are her safety net. I am asking you for your own good to cut that net and move on with your life. She won't bring you happiness."

Mitch stood by the sink looking at the window; they could hear Mac and Faith still arguing. "They will be like this for hours, she drove us to distraction in her younger days. When John came on the scene and took her away, yes, we were sad, but then we got our lives back. I think it's time we set the table," Mitch nodded. "I am coming and thank you Mary for being honest."

Mary just smiled but felt like a heel and knew she just broke the heart of a very nice, sensible man but knew it had to be done, for his own sake. They both went back into the dining room and set the table. "Will you two pack it in, I am fed up with it," said Mary.

"I will go tell the boys to clean up," said Mitch. Mary looked up at him as he went to the back door and went out to the boys.

That evening, they all sat playing twister and Pictionary until it was time for the boys to go to bed. Mac got out the red wine with four glasses and poured. They talked and drank till midnight.

Faith didn't ask Jake if he wanted to come back with them. Instead, she hugged, squeezed and kissed him. She hugged her parents. "You have done the right thing, sweetheart," said Mary. Faith tearful and nodding, walked to the car and got in. The boys said their goodbyes and got in the car.

Mitch was the last to say goodbye, he kissed Mary on the cheek. "Thank you, both of you," and shook Mac's hand. "I don't think I will be seeing you both again, take care of yourselves."

"Mitch, we really wish things could be different. Take care of yourself," Mac and Mary watched them drive away whilst Jake said his goodbyes then went to see Ella.

Chapter 24

A week had passed and Mark and Henry were itching to see their dad, whilst Matthew wouldn't see him and stayed with Mitch. Faith got the boys into the car, then drove to the farm.

Mark and Henry were excited as they approached the farm. They could see the guys working in the fields, waving as they went by but unsure if anyone actually saw them or not. Faith parked the car, "Mummy, Mummy, I can see George and Daddy in the top field. May we go to them?"

"Yes, but be careful. Tell your dad I will be in the kitchen."

The boys jumped out of the car and ran towards their father and George. John waved back at them and then ran towards the boys and wrapped both of them up in his arms swinging them around in a circle, with both boys laughing hysterically, asking for more. He wrestled with them to the ground then both of them jumped on top of him.

George walked over and had a wrestle himself with the boys, placing Mark on his shoulders and Henry under one arm, taking them to the tractor and putting them in the cab. John dusted himself down and headed to the house, anxious to see Faith.

Faith was surprised at the cleanliness of the house although rather sparse. She put on the kettle and made two coffees. "You're back then; how are your parents and how was Jake?"

"They are all fine. I see you cleaned the house or did you get someone in to do it for you?"

"No, I did it," John said, sitting down at the make shift table.

"You look better than you did a week ago. What's with the change?"

"I've been dry for just over a week now and I have been to an AA meeting as well."

"Babe, that's great," Faith said, placing her hand in his squeezing it tight.

"I also have an appointment to see a shrink."

"What's with this sudden change of direction?"

"I want my life back, and I want my family back. Its early stages but I have never been more determined about anything. I am not saying I am not going to have relapses, but I am just going to take one step at a time."

"And we will be with you every step of the way."

"I take it Matthew didn't want to come."

"He is still upset; give him time, he will come to you when he is ready. So what are you going to do with the place now it's pretty much a blank canvas?"

"I was hoping we could do it together."

"Sounds good to me."

"I know what the boys want so I will start with their rooms first."

"Oh, John."

"It will keep me busy."

John and Faith spoke a great deal about the present, their future wants and needs, not realising the time. "Listen I have to go, the boys are still with George."

"No worries, I will drop them off later and I will feed them two hungry horses as well if you like?"

"Oh, that sounds great."

"Well, I will see you later then."

As she walked off John took her hand and pulled her back to him, locked her in an embrace. "I mean what I say; I want my family back," he kissed her on the lips.

Later that evening the boys were in bed, Mitch lit the fire and Faith made baileys hot chocolate for them both. "How did it go this afternoon at the farm?"

"Okay, I guess. John has gone to an AA meeting and has an appointment with a shrink next week, I think."

"Listen Faith, I have come to a decision. I am leaving, moving away to Tasmania."

"What about me and the boys? What's going to happen to us, they are just starting to get settled?"

"The truth is they will never be settled here because this isn't their home. When we spoke a few weeks ago, I said we would stay as friends. I was just kidding myself; I want more, I want more from you but I know you cannot give me what I want because the truth is you have never left John, you're still in love with him."

"I do love you."

"But not in the way I want you to love me."

"I'm sorry."

"Don't be, I just hoped that you would feel the same about me. I have loved you for so long; I lost sight of what really matters to me because I have been so consumed with you."

"We will move out tomorrow."

"There is no need to, really. Stay. I will be flying down on Sunday for a few days to check out houses and things, so you have a while yet, to get things sorted with John."

"I'm sorry."

"Again, don't be. I'm going to bed. See you in the morning."

***

Jake was at the abandoned warehouse by himself. He put together scraps of wood, paper and any other materials that would burn and then set them alight, the flames burned with colour each flare was irresistible appearing majestic consuming whatever it pleased, it had no mind and held no pity. It burned hot and violent. The flames flickered and danced, touched his insides, feeling alive and consumed, he could hear the echoes in the woods, carried on the breeze engulfing and swirling around him.

Their voices calling his name, seeing their faces burning in the flames, one by one they looked into his soul as he consumed them in death, the sweet feeling, he found intoxicating. Driven by the obsessive fantasy, reliving the events in a trance-like state; as he masturbated, the anger and rage built within him. Exploding his seed into the fire, his smile turned to a pleasing grimace allowing the feeling of empowerment settle into his core.

Over the coming weeks and months he became more isolated. Other than his kickboxing lessons, he saw less and less of his friends; he only gave Ella his full attention. It was her and him, against the world. As they grew, his increasing appetite and sexual desire towards her increased, he had taken photos of her and would masturbate obsessively over them imagining her tied up and him, drinking her blood.

In his mind, he didn't need nor want anyone else. As long as he was with Ella nothing else mattered, they were joined in mind and body. Their first time together in an adult way was truly exceptional, they would be together in their safe space, their den, his fantasies with her were starting to come true.